TAPE & GLUE

A NOVEL

THE PIECES SERIES
BOOK 2

S. SWISS

SWISS HOUSE PUBLISHING

CONTENTS

First Edition

Cover design by S.Swiss

Swiss House Publishing

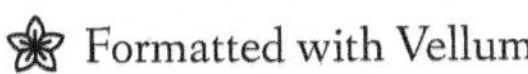 Formatted with Vellum

For my husband,
Who put back together the pieces
Of a heart he didn't break

And for my friends and Family—
For staying, loving, and never letting go

THE PIECES SERIES

ONE

AFTER

Two months had passed.

Long enough that I should've felt better. Long enough that I should've felt like myself again.

I didn't.

From the outside, I probably looked fine.

I was going out again. Saying yes to everything. Bars.

House parties. Anywhere loud enough to drown things out.

Music too loud. Drinks too strong. People too close.

It helped, until it didn't. Because the second it got quiet, he was still there. So I kept it loud.

Guys were different now.

Or maybe I was.

They weren't hard to read. They just didn't matter.

I laughed when I was supposed to. Flirted when it was easy. Kept everything surface-level. Nothing real. Nothing that could turn into something. Sometimes I let it go further.

A kiss in the corner of a bar. Hands where they didn't belong.

Just enough to feel something. Or maybe just enough to prove I still could.

But it never lasted.

Because the second their hands moved too fast, or held on too long, my body reacted before my mind could catch up.

Tensing. Pulling back. Heart racing like something was wrong, even when I couldn't explain why.

I'd laugh it off. Make a joke. Blame the alcohol.

Step away like it was nothing.

But it wasn't nothing.

Something about it felt wrong now. Not them.

Just everything.

Like I couldn't tell the difference anymore between normal and too much. Between attention and pressure. Between what I wanted and what I had learned to go along with.

So I stopped trying to figure it out.

It was easier that way.

"Okay, that guy was definitely into you,"

Lo said, leaning in close over the music.

I glanced back.

He was still watching. Waiting.

I shrugged. "So?"

She frowned a little. "You used to care about that."

I took another drink. "Not anymore."

And I meant it.

At least, I wanted to.

Miles still texted me.

Not constantly. But enough.

You okay?

Be safe.

Miss you.

Familiar. Easy.

There was a time when he felt like everything.

I had loved him for so long. In a way that felt steady. Safe.

But safe hadn't been enough.

Or maybe it had just never been fully mine.

We were still something.

Friends, if that's what you called it.

Flirty sometimes. Comfortable. Like slipping into something that didn't fit the same way anymore.

I didn't see him like that now. Didn't feel it the way I used to.

And part of me didn't trust it anymore anyway.

Because I wasn't sure I trusted anything.

Not what I felt. Not what I wanted. Not what something was supposed to be.

"Earth to Anna."

Lo nudged my shoulder. "You're doing it again."

"Doing what?"

"Leaving."

I blinked at her. "I'm here."

She gave me a look. "Physically."

I forced a small smile. "I'm fine."

She didn't believe me. I didn't blame her.

Later that night, I stepped outside.

Cool air. Quieter.

The kind of moment that used to calm me down.

Now it just made everything louder in my head.

I leaned against the railing and stared out into nothing, trying to feel normal. Trying to feel anything that made sense.

My phone buzzed.

I almost ignored it.

But I didn't.

I looked down.

Stephen.

My stomach dropped.

Sharp. Immediate.

I hadn't seen his name in weeks. Not since everything.

My thumb hovered over the screen.

Then I opened it.

I still love you.

That was it.

No explanation. No apology. Nothing that made it make sense.

Just that.

My chest tightened.

Not soft. Not warm.

Familiar.

Like my body remembered him before my mind could stop it.

I should've ignored it. I knew that.

But I didn't.

You shouldn't text me.

The three dots appeared instantly.

Of course they did.

Because that was how it always worked.

I closed my eyes for a second, gripping my phone tighter than I meant to.

Two months.

Two months of trying to put myself back together. Of

pretending I was okay. Of not thinking about him, or what he had done.

And all it took was one message.

"Who is it?" Lo's voice came from behind me.

I turned my phone over too fast. "No one."

She raised an eyebrow.

Didn't push.

Thank God.

Because I didn't have an answer.

I looked back down at the screen.

At his name.

At the message still sitting there.

I still love you.

My chest tightened again.

Because the truth was, I wasn't over him.

Not even close.

And I hated that.

I typed slowly.

Stopped.

Deleted it.

Tried again.

Then finally:

I can't do this again.

Sent.

And even as the message delivered, I knew.

That wasn't the end.

Because no matter how many nights I went out, no matter how loud I made everything, no matter how many people I let get close just to prove I could—

there was still a part of me that couldn't tell the difference between love and what he did to me.

And that part was the one that still missed him.

My fingers tightened around my phone.

Like if I held on hard enough, I wouldn't reach for him again.

TWO

WHAT'S LEFT BEHIND

The Uber ride felt longer than it should have.

Or maybe it was just quieter.

The music from earlier still rang faintly in my ears — laughter, voices, the kind of noise that made everything feel manageable.

Out here, there was nothing.

Just the hum of the road.

Streetlights passing across the window.

My reflection staring back at me in the glass.

I didn't recognize her like this. Not fully.

"You good back there?" the driver asked.

"Yeah," I said quickly.

Too quickly.

. . .

I turned my head and watched the street blur past instead, counting turns, landmarks, anything that made it feel like I was getting somewhere.

Because for the first time in weeks, I was going home alone.

No Lo.

No one on the couch.

No voices in the other room to fill the space.

Just me.

The car slowed, then stopped.

My building came into view.

The same one I had pulled up to a hundred times before.

Nothing about it looked different. But my chest still tightened.

"Here you go," the driver said.

"Thanks."

I stepped out quickly, pulling my jacket tighter around me as the car drove off. The second it disappeared, the silence hit.

Too quiet.

I stood there for a second longer than I meant to, just looking at the building like I was waiting for something to feel familiar.

It didn't.

The walk to my door felt longer than it used to.

Every step louder. Every sound sharper.

My keys shook slightly in my hand as I unlocked the door.

The second I stepped inside, Bella came running.

Nails clicking against the floor.

Tail wagging like nothing in the world had ever been wrong.

"Hey," I whispered, crouching down as she pressed into me.

Warm.

Real.

I held onto her a second longer than I needed to.

"You're okay," I murmured.

More for me than for her.

She didn't question anything.

Didn't notice anything different.

She just stayed.

I stood slowly and closed the door behind me.

The apartment was quiet.

Too quiet.

Clean.

Put back together.

The table replaced.

The walls fixed.

Everything exactly how it was supposed to be.

And still, it didn't feel right.

Because no matter how much had been repaired, I could still see it.

The way it looked that night.

The way it sounded.

The way it felt.

Like it had soaked into everything.

I moved through the space slowly, like if I went too fast, I'd run into it.

The couch.

The hallway.

The kitchen.

All of it the same.

All of it different.

. . .

I exhaled and forced myself to keep moving.

My bedroom felt smaller than I remembered.

Safer.

But only because I had convinced myself it was.

I crossed to the closet and dropped my bag on the floor before kneeling down.

I pushed aside a pair of shoes.

Then another.

Until I reached it.

The box.

Simple.

Worn at the edges.

I hadn't touched it in weeks.

I didn't need to open it to know what was there.

The letters.

Every one of them from him.

Two months.

Two months of words I hadn't been ready to read.

I sat back on my heels and stared at it.

My phone buzzed faintly from somewhere behind me.

I ignored it.

Because I already knew.

I had spent weeks trying not to think about him.

Not to feel it.

Not to go back there.

And tonight, for some reason, that felt impossible.

I reached for the box slowly.

Hesitated.

Just for a second.

Then pulled the lid off.

The letters were stacked neatly inside.

Folded.

Ordered.

Like they meant something.

Like he meant them.

My fingers hovered over the top one.

I knew I shouldn't.

I knew exactly what this was.

The same pull.

The same feeling.

The one I kept pretending I was past.

But the truth was, I hadn't been able to stop thinking about him since the message.

I still love you.

My chest tightened again.

I picked up the first letter and held it there.

For a second, I just stared at it.

Because opening it meant letting him back in.

And I didn't know if I was strong enough to keep him out after that.

But my fingers moved anyway.

Because they always did.

Anna,

I don't even know where to start.

I've rewritten this more times than I can count, and none of it feels like enough. Nothing I say is going to undo what happened. I know that. I have to live with that.

But I need you to hear this from me—

I am so sorry.

Not in the way people say it when they're trying to move on.

Not in the way that makes it easier.

I'm sorry in the way that keeps me up at night replaying everything over and over again, wishing I could go back and be someone different in that moment.

You didn't deserve that.

You didn't deserve any of it.

And I hate myself for being the person who did that to you.

I know you probably don't want to hear from me. You shouldn't have to.

But pretending you don't exist, pretending we didn't have what we had... I can't do that. I won't.

Because it was real to me, Anna.

You were real to me.

Everything we had—every late night, every laugh, every moment where it felt like the rest of the world didn't exist—that wasn't fake. That wasn't nothing.

And I know I don't get to ask anything from you.

I know I don't deserve your time, your forgiveness... or even a response.

But I need you to know I'm trying to be better.

I've been thinking a lot about everything—about myself, about the way I handle things, about how I let it get that far. I don't want to be that person again. I don't want to hurt you... or anyone... like that ever again.

You mattered too much to me for that to be the way things ended.

I miss you.

More than I should probably admit.

Not just having you in my life... but you.

The way you understood me. The way you saw me when no one else did.

I know I don't get to ask for another chance.

I know I don't deserve it.

But if there's even a small part of you that remembers what we were...

if there's any part of you that believes I can be better—

I hope one day you might let me prove that

to you.
If not… I understand.
I just needed you to know that I'm sorry.
And that losing you is something I'll regret for the rest of my life.
—Stephen

I shouldn't have opened it.

I knew that before I even unfolded the paper.

Knew it in the way my hands shook… in the way my chest tightened before I read a single word.

Still—

I did.

Anna,

My stomach dropped.

Just seeing my name in his handwriting was enough to pull me back.

Back to everything I've been trying not to think about.

Back to him.

I told myself I wouldn't read the whole thing.

Just the first line.

Just enough to know what it was.

But then my eyes kept moving.

Line after line.

Word after word.

I'm sorry.

My jaw tightened.

Of course he was.

Of course that's how it started.

My grip on the paper tightened, the edges crinkling between my fingers as I kept reading. My heart was beating too fast—like it didn't know if it was supposed to run or stay.

You didn't deserve that.

A breath caught in my throat.

Because that part—

that part was true.

And I hated that it was true.

Hated that he could say something right... and it still didn't make anything better.

I swallowed hard, forcing myself to keep going.

It was real to me, Anna.

My chest ached.

I squeezed my eyes shut for a second, but it didn't stop it.

Didn't stop the memories from slipping in anyway.

The late nights.

The way he used to look at me like I was the only thing that mattered.

The feeling of being chosen.

My fingers loosened slightly on the paper.

That was the dangerous part.

Not the apology.

Not even the regret.

It was that.

The way he could take something broken...

and make me remember the pieces that felt whole.

I opened my eyes again, forcing myself to finish.

I miss you.

A sharp breath left my chest.

"No," I whispered, shaking my head like I could physically push the words away.

No.

I folded the letter halfway—then stopped.

Because I hadn't reached the end.

And for some reason...

that mattered.

My hands were trembling now.

I didn't want to care.

Didn't want to feel anything reading his words.

But I did.

I hated that I did.

I read the last lines slower.

If there's even a small part of you...

My chest tightened again.

Because there was.

That was the truth I didn't want to look at too closely.

There was a part of me that remembered him before everything went wrong.

A part of me that still felt something when I saw his name.

And that part of me—

terrified me.

I let the paper fall into my lap, staring at it like it might say something else if I looked long enough.

Like it might take it all back.

It didn't.

It just sat there.

Heavy.

Too heavy for something that was only a few pages long.

I should throw it away.

I knew that.

Knew it the same way I knew I shouldn't have opened it in the first place.

But I didn't move.

Didn't reach for the trash.

Didn't tear it up.

Instead...

I smoothed it out with my hands.

Careful.

Like it was something fragile.

And that was the moment I realized—

This wasn't over.

Not for him.

And not for me either.

THREE
THE SECOND LETTER

I didn't move right away.

The first letter still sat in my hands, the paper slightly creased where my fingers had tightened around it.

I should've put it back. Closed the box. Left it there.

But I didn't.

My phone sat beside me on the bed, face down, waiting.

I stared at it longer than I meant to.

Then, slowly, I picked it up.

Unlocked it.

His message was still there.

I still love you.

My chest tightened again.

Not softer this time.

Heavier.

My fingers hovered over the screen.

I could end it right here.

One message.

That's all it would take.

Don't contact me again.

This is over.

You don't get to do this.

The words came easily in my head. Clear. Certain.

But when I tried to type them, my hands didn't move.

Because it didn't feel that simple. Because part of me — the part I didn't want to admit was still there — hesitated.

What if he meant it? What if he really was sorry?

What if—

I squeezed my eyes shut.

No.

I knew better than that.

I had to know better than that.

Still, my thumb moved.

I...

The single letter sat there on the screen.

Waiting.

I stared at it.

Then quickly deleted it.

Locked my phone.

Turned it over.

Like that would make it stop.

Like that would make him stop.

It didn't.

Because he was still there.

In the room.

In my head.

In the way my chest still hadn't settled.

I exhaled slowly and reached back into the box.

The second letter sat right beneath the first.

I hesitated longer this time.

Then pulled it out anyway.

Unfolded it.

Anna,

My chest tightened instantly.

I know you're probably reading this and trying to convince your-self I don't deserve another chance.

My stomach dropped.

And maybe I don't.

But you don't just stop loving someone like me.

Not after everything we had.

My breath caught.

The words felt different this time.

Less careful.

Sharper.

I know you. Better than anyone. And I know how your mind works. You're overthinking this. You always do.

My fingers tightened around the page.

You're going to let everyone else get in your head. Your friends. Your family. People who weren't there.

I shook my head slightly.

They're going to make me the bad guy. They already are.

The words blurred for a second.

But you know I'm not. Not really.

My chest tightened harder.

You saw me at my worst. I know that. But that doesn't erase everything else.

My eyes moved slower now.

And if you're being honest with yourself—

I stopped.

Something about that line felt different.

Heavier.

Like I already knew where it was going.

you weren't exactly innocent in it either.

The words hit harder than they should have.

My stomach twisted.

No.

I swallowed.

No.

I dropped the letter into my lap.

My chest tightened faster now.

That feeling I hadn't been able to name before rushed in all at once.

Wrong.

This felt wrong.

But my body didn't slow down.

It sped up.

My breathing quickened.

My hands started to shake.

Then —

SLAM.

The sound came from somewhere outside.

A door. A car. Something loud enough to cut through everything.

But my body didn't care what it was.

I flinched hard.

My heart jumped into my throat, panic rising too fast to catch.

For a second, I wasn't in my room anymore.

I was back there.

The noise.

The walls.

The way everything felt right before it got worse.

"No—"

My voice came out shaky.

Too quiet.

I pushed the letters off my lap like it burned.

My chest heaving now.

Breath uneven.

Too fast.

"It's fine," I whispered.

"It's fine."

But it didn't feel fine.

Nothing felt fine.

I pulled my knees to my chest and pressed my hands against my face, trying to slow it down, trying to make it stop.

But it didn't.

Because it wasn't just the sound.

It was everything.

The letters.

The message.

His voice in my head, twisting things just enough to make me question myself again.

I shook my head and squeezed my eyes shut.

"No," I whispered again.

Like saying it out loud would make it true.

Eventually, the panic softened.

Not gone.

Just quieter.

Exhaustion settled in where it had been, heavy.

I lowered myself back onto the bed slowly and turned onto my side.

Bella shifted beside me and pressed closer.

I reached for her without thinking, holding onto something that felt real.

Safe.

My eyes burned.

And this time, I didn't try to stop it.

The tears came quietly.

Not sharp.

Not loud.

Just steady.

Like everything I had been holding in finally had somewhere to go.

I stared at the wall, the room dark around me again.

The letters still scattered on the bed behind me.

Unread.

Unfinished.

But already too much.

My breathing slowed eventually.

My body finally giving in to the exhaustion.

And somewhere between the tears and the quiet, I fell asleep.

Not because I felt better.

Just because I didn't have anything left in me to stay awake.

FOUR
THE IN BETWEEN

I didn't answer right away.

I stared at the message longer than I should have.

I need to see you.

Please.

My chest tightened.

Not sharp.

Familiar.

I knew what I was supposed to do.

Ignore it.

Block him.

Tell someone.

I didn't.

My fingers moved anyway.

Okay.

A pause.

Tonight.

Another pause.

Don't text me again until I'm ready.

I stared at the message after I sent it, like I could take it back.

I couldn't.

Because part of me had already decided.

By the time Caleb knocked, I had already convinced myself I was fine.

"Hey," he said, holding up a coffee in one hand and a dog bone in the other. "For Bella."

I smiled despite myself.

"You're her favorite already."

Bella ran to him immediately, nails clicking against the floor, tail wagging like nothing in the world had ever gone wrong.

"Yeah, I can tell," he laughed, crouching down to greet her.

Caleb felt easy.

Familiar in a way that didn't make my chest tight.

Didn't make me question everything.

He knew me from before.

Before everything got complicated.

Before I did.

"You ready?" he asked, standing.

"Yeah."

We took Bella for a walk first.

The air was cool, the neighborhood quiet in that normal, almost forgettable way.

We talked about nothing.

High school.

People we used to know.

Stories that didn't matter.

And for a little while, it felt okay.

Not exciting.

Not intense.

Just safe.

We stopped at a small store after, grabbing snacks we didn't need.

Laughing about something stupid.

And for a second, I almost forgot.

Almost.

Because every once in a while, my mind drifted.

To later.

To him.

To the fact that I had already said yes.

"You're quiet," Caleb said, nudging me lightly.

"I'm just tired."

He nodded. Didn't push.

That was the thing about him.

He didn't push.

And I didn't know what to do with that.

By the time we got back to my apartment, the sun had shifted lower.

Later now.

Closer to evening.

Caleb sat on the couch, Bella curled up beside him like she had known him forever.

"You good?" he asked.

I nodded.

"Yeah."

And for a second, I almost told him.

About the message.

About tonight.

But I didn't.

Because saying it out loud would've made it real.

He left not long after.

A quick hug.

Easy.

"I'll see you soon?" he asked.

I smiled.

"Yeah."

And I meant it.

At least part of me did.

The apartment felt different after he left.

Quieter.

Heavier.

I moved through it slowly, my chest tightening with every passing minute.

Because now there was nothing left to distract me.

Just time.

And the decision I had already made.

When Stephen finally showed up, everything shifted.

The second I opened the door, it was like nothing had changed.

And everything had.

"Hey," he said.

Just that.

Like we hadn't broken anything between us.

"It's weird seeing you," I admitted.

"Yeah," he said quietly.

A pause.

Then he stepped inside.

And just like that, the space felt smaller.

Tighter.

We didn't talk much at first.

Didn't need to.

Because the tension was already there.

Sitting between us.

Waiting.

"You look good," he said.

My chest tightened.

I hesitated, lifting my hand to my hair.

"I cut it."

His eyes moved over me again.

Taking it in.

"It looks good," he said.

Softer this time.

Something about the way he said it — like he saw the change but didn't really understand it — made something in my chest tighten even more.

Because I hadn't cut it for him.

I had cut it because I needed something to feel different.

Something I could control.

Something that felt like mine again.

"Don't," I said quietly.

But I didn't step back.

The distance between us closed slowly.

Not rushed.

Not forced.

Just inevitable.

And even though part of me knew I should stop, I didn't.

Because it felt unfinished.

Like something I hadn't been able to let go of.

And when it happened, it wasn't soft.

It wasn't careful.

It was intense.

Heavy.

Like both of us had been holding onto something we didn't know how to release.

And somewhere in the middle of it, my eyes burned.

Tears slipped down quietly.

Not because it felt right.

But because it didn't.

Because I knew.

I knew this wasn't right.

I knew this wasn't what moving on looked like.

But I also knew I still loved him.

And my body hadn't caught up to everything my mind was trying to understand.

Later, everything slowed.

The room quiet again.

Too quiet.

I lay there staring at the ceiling, my chest still uneven.

Stephen's arm rested across me.

Familiar.

Like we hadn't just crossed that line again.

"You okay?" he murmured.

I nodded.

Because I didn't know what else to do.

Morning came faster than it should have.

My phone buzzed beside me.

Lo.

I'm stopping by.

My chest tightened instantly.

I sat up quickly.

"You have to go."

Stephen frowned slightly.

"What?"

"Lo's coming."

A pause.

He didn't move right away.

Like he didn't want to.

Then slowly, he sat up.

"Okay," he said.

But something in his expression lingered.

Like this wasn't over.

He pulled his shirt back on, glancing at me one more time.

"I'll come back tonight," he said.

Not a question.

"If you let me."

I didn't answer.

Because I didn't know what the answer was.

And that scared me more than anything.

Because part of me had already said yes.

FIVE
THE SPLIT

The sound of the sliding door was quiet.

Too quiet.

Stephen moved carefully, pulling his shirt over his head as he stepped out onto the patio.

"Text me," he said, low.

I didn't answer.

Because I didn't know if I would.

The door slid shut behind him with a soft click.

And just like that, it was like he had never been there.

Except he had.

My chest hadn't caught up yet.

A knock sounded at the front door.

Sharp. Immediate.

"Anna?" Lo's voice called.

I froze for half a second.

Then moved.

"Coming," I said, forcing my voice steady as I walked through the apartment.

I opened the door.

Lo stepped in immediately, her eyes scanning me, then the space behind me.

"You look like you just woke up," she said.

"I did."

She studied me longer than usual.

"Were you alone?"

The question landed heavier than it should have.

"Yeah," I said.

Too quickly.

Her eyes didn't move.

But she didn't push.

"Okay," she said finally.

It didn't sound like she believed me.

We spent the day together, out of the apartment.

Coffee first.

Then walking around downtown.

Then nothing in particular — just moving from one place to another, filling the hours.

Lo talked about everything.

Work.

Friends.

Plans I half-listened to.

And I nodded.

Laughed when I was supposed to.

Because it was easier than sitting still.

Easier than thinking.

"You seem... better," she said at one point, glancing over at me.

"I am," I said.

And part of me meant it.

At least the part of me that was trying.

By the time evening rolled around, I was back at my apartment.

The quiet felt different now.

Less heavy.

Or maybe I was just better at ignoring it.

A knock came at the door.

Caleb.

He stood there holding a takeout bag in one hand and a bottle of wine in the other.

"I come bearing gifts," he said.

I smiled, stepping aside to let him in.

"What is it?"

"Your favorite," he said. "That salad from the pizza place you wouldn't shut up about."

I laughed.

"You remembered that?"

"Yeah," he said simply.

Like remembering things about me was just something he did.

Not something I had to earn.

We ate on the couch.

Bella curled up between us, perfectly content.

The TV played something neither of us was really watching.

And for a while, everything felt normal.

Not forced.

Not intense.

Just easy.

Caleb leaned back slightly, his arm brushing mine.

Not pulling me in.

Not holding me there.

Just there.

And for the first time in a while, I didn't feel like I had to think about it.

I just let it be.

"You okay?" he asked quietly.

I nodded.

"Yeah."

And this time, it felt closer to true.

At some point, we both drifted off.

The room dim.

The TV still playing softly.

His shoulder warm beside mine.

Safe.

I woke up to my phone buzzing.

Again.

And again.

And again.

My chest tightened before I even picked it up.

Stephen.

Missed texts.

More than I wanted to count.

Where are you?

Why aren't you answering me?

I thought you said you'd see me tonight.

Anna.

Answer me.

My stomach dropped.

The shift was immediate.

That same feeling.

Tight.

Heavy.

Like I had done something wrong, even though I hadn't.

I glanced over.

Caleb was still asleep beside me.

Peaceful.

Unaware.

I looked back down at my phone.

My fingers hovered.

Then I typed:

I can't tonight.

Sent.

A pause.

Then nothing.

For a second, I thought that was it.

That it would just end there.

It didn't.

The next day felt almost normal.

Too normal.

Coffee again.

Errands.

Running into people I hadn't seen in a while.

Old friends.

People who knew me.

Who knew him.

And every once in a while, I caught it.

The looks.

The questions they didn't ask out loud.

"You're doing better," one of them said.

I nodded.

"Yeah."

Caleb stayed close.

Easy.

Familiar.

Like he had always been there.

And part of me leaned into that.

Because it felt like something I could hold onto without losing myself.

By that night, I hadn't heard from Stephen again.

Not since the messages.

Not since I didn't show up.

It should've felt like relief.

Instead, it felt like something waiting.

Then my phone buzzed.

A message from someone else.

He asked about you.

My chest tightened instantly.

Stephen.

A pause.

Then:

He knows you've been seeing someone.

I stared at the screen.

My stomach dropping slowly.

Because I knew exactly what that meant.

Stephen knew.

About Caleb.

About me not showing up.

About everything.

And Stephen was not the kind of person who let things go.

SIX

UNANNOUNCED

The knock wasn't loud.

But it didn't need to be.

I knew.

Before I even looked at the door, I knew.

My chest tightened instantly.

That same drop. That same feeling.

I moved slowly, my feet heavier than they should've been. When I opened it, Stephen stood there.

Like nothing had changed.

"Hey," he said.

Just that.

Like showing up uninvited was normal.

"What are you doing here?" I asked.

"You didn't answer me," he said simply.

Not angry.

Not yet.

Just there.

He stepped past me before I could say anything else.

And just like that, he was inside.

The door shut behind him.

The apartment felt smaller immediately.

His eyes moved around the space.

The empty wine bottle on the counter.

The crumpled takeout bag.

From last night.

From Caleb.

My stomach dropped.

Stephen didn't say anything at first. Just looked.

Then I said, quietly, "Don't."

But I didn't step back.

The distance between us closed slowly.

Not rushed.

Not forced.

Just familiar.

And that was the problem.

Because my body remembered him before anything else did.

His hand found my waist.

Steady.

Grounding.

Pulling me closer like it had a hundred times before.

I should've stopped it.

I felt that.

But the moment didn't feel like a decision.

It felt like something I had already stepped into. Something I didn't know how to step out of without making it worse.

So I didn't.

I let him pull me in.

Not because I wanted to.

Not fully.

But because resisting him right then didn't feel safe either.

For a second, it almost felt like before.

Familiar.

Close.

Until it didn't.

Until I felt it.

That shift.

The way his grip stayed just a little too firm.

The way the moment wasn't really mine anymore.

By the time it ended, my chest felt tight.

My thoughts slower than they should've been.

I pulled away first this time.

Grabbed a T-shirt and pulled it over my head quickly, like I needed something between me and him. Something to cover the way I suddenly felt exposed.

Stephen didn't move right away.

He just watched me.

And that's when it changed.

"You had someone here," he said.

Not a question.

My stomach dropped.

And just like that, whatever that moment had been was gone.

Replaced with something colder.

Something tighter.

"Busy night?" he added.

Light.

Too light.

"It was nothing," I said.

He nodded slowly.

But his eyes flicked toward the counter.

The wine bottle.

The takeout bag.

"Looks like something."

The words sat heavier this time.

And suddenly I felt it.

Not just the room getting smaller.

But the realization that I had just let my guard down at the exact moment I shouldn't have.

"You didn't come see me," he said.

"I told you I couldn't."

"You said tonight."

My chest tightened again.

"I changed my mind."

A pause.

His jaw shifted slightly.

Then a small smile.

"Yeah," he said. "Seems like you did."

The way he said it made something in my stomach twist.

"I'm not doing this," I said, shaking my head slightly. "You should leave."

He didn't move.

Instead, his hand found my arm.

Firm.

"Relax," he said quietly.

My body stiffened instantly.

"Stephen—"

"I'm not here to fight," he said.

But his grip didn't loosen.

"I just wanted to see you."

The words didn't match the way it felt.

Not even close.

He pulled me slightly toward him.

Not enough to drag.

Not enough to leave a mark.

Just enough to make it clear he wasn't asking.

My heart started to race.

"Stephen, you need to go."

His expression shifted, just slightly.

His grip tightened.

"Who was it?"

"It doesn't matter."

"It does to me."

The words landed heavier this time.

And suddenly it wasn't about the wine.

Or the food.

It was about control.

"I said it doesn't matter."

He stared at me.

Then, "Caleb?"

My stomach dropped.

The room felt smaller.

"How do you—"

"I've heard things," he said.

His voice stayed calm.

Too calm.

"You think I wouldn't find out?"

My heart was racing now.

Because it wasn't just what he was saying.

It was how easily he said it.

Like it was expected.

"Stephen, stop," I said.

But my voice didn't sound strong.

It sounded small.

His hand slid from my arm to my waist.

Pulling me closer.

"Did he stay here?" he asked quietly.

My chest tightened.

"Answer me."

The pressure in his voice — low, controlled — made my stomach twist.

I didn't answer.

Because suddenly all I could think about was Caleb.

About him showing up again.

About Stephen seeing him.

Finding him.

Something in my chest dropped.

"You don't need him," Stephen said.

Like that settled it.

Like that was the end of the conversation.

"I'm serious," I said, pulling back slightly. "You need to leave."

This time, he didn't smile.

For a second, something darker flickered across his face.

Then just as quickly, it was gone.

"Alright," he said.

Like it was nothing.

Like he hadn't just—

"Go take a shower," he added, turning toward the bathroom.

I blinked.

"What?"

"You've got work, right?" he said casually, turning the water on. "You don't have to worry. I'm not going to stay."

My chest tightened.

Nothing about this felt right.

But the water was already running.

The room already shifting again.

And for some reason, I hesitated.

Because pushing him further didn't feel safe either.

"Just get ready," he said, glancing back at me. "I'll go."

I swallowed.

Then slowly moved toward the bathroom.

Because right now, keeping things calm felt like the only option.

The water hit my skin, hot enough to ground me.

For a second, I let myself breathe.

Let myself believe he would leave.

That this would end.

Then the curtain moved.

My heart jumped.

Stephen stepped in like it was nothing.

Like he belonged there.

"Stephen—"

"Relax," he murmured again.

His hands found me immediately.

Familiar.

Too familiar.

Pulling me into him.

Claiming space that wasn't his anymore.

My chest tightened.

I should've stopped it.

I knew that.

I felt that.

But my body betrayed me.

Reacted anyway.

Because it was easier.

Because fighting him didn't feel safe.

Because part of me still hadn't untangled what this was supposed to feel like.

So I didn't fight it.

I just went still.

Let it happen.

After, I moved quickly.

Out of the shower.

Pulling on the first T-shirt I could find.

My hands weren't steady.

My thoughts weren't either.

Because now I knew.

This couldn't keep happening.

Not like this.

"I'm leaving," I said.

Stephen nodded.

Like that was expected.

"I'll see you tonight," he said.

Not a question.

My chest tightened again.

I didn't answer.

The second I got in my car, I didn't go to work.

I couldn't.

Instead, I drove.

Straight to Lexie's.

My hands still shaking on the wheel.

My chest still tight.

When I walked in, Lexie looked up immediately.

"Anna?"

Mallory was there too.

Boxes stacked around them.

Half-packed.

Half-finished.

"You're early," Mallory said.

I didn't answer.

Because the second I opened my mouth, everything came out.

All of it.

The letters.

The messages.

Him showing up.

The way it felt.

The way I didn't stop it.

The way I couldn't.

"I feel so stupid," I said finally, my voice breaking. "I almost let myself fall back into it."

Lexie shook her head immediately.

"No," she said.

"You didn't. You came here."

My chest tightened.

"You're leaving in two days," Mallory said softly. "He doesn't know that."

The words landed slowly.

A way out.

A real one.

"I can't keep doing this," I said.

And for the first time, it felt true.

Not just something I was saying.

Something I meant.

"I have to end it," I added quietly.

My chest tightened again.

Because I knew.

That didn't just mean Stephen.

It meant everything.

Even Caleb.

Because right now, I wasn't safe.

And neither was anyone close to me.

For the first time in weeks, I wasn't thinking about going back.

I was thinking about getting out.

SEVEN
LETTING GO OF THE EASY

Lexie didn't let me leave right away.

"You're not going back there tonight," she said.

There wasn't even a question in it.

That was the thing about Lexie.

She had never been unsure about me.

Not once.

Not before everything.

Not after.

She had just stayed.

Through all of it.

The nights I didn't answer.

The things I didn't say out loud.

The version of me I didn't even recognize anymore.

She was still there.

Always.

Lexie leaned against the kitchen counter, arms crossed, watching me like she was making sure I didn't change my mind.

She looked exactly how she always did.

Effortless.

Tall. Put together. The kind of naturally beautiful people noticed without her ever trying.

But that wasn't what made her who she was.

It was the way she showed up.

The way she never judged.

Never made me feel less than.

Never made me question if I could come to her.

She was steady.

Safe.

Everything you would want in a friend — and somehow, I had never had to wonder if she'd stay.

"You can stay here," she said again, softer this time.

I nodded.

Because for the first time in a while, going back didn't feel like an option.

The next morning came too fast.

Not because I had slept well.

Because I hadn't.

My phone sat beside me on the couch.

Silent.

I hadn't answered him.

Not last night.

Not this morning.

And for once, I didn't reach for it.

Instead, I texted Caleb.

Can we talk?

He responded almost immediately.

Yeah. Everything okay?

My chest tightened.

I didn't answer that part.

Can you come by?

He showed up within the hour.

Same as always.

Easy.

Like nothing had changed.

But everything had.

"Hey," he said, stepping inside.

I didn't hug him.

Didn't move closer.

And I think he noticed.

"You okay?" he asked.

I nodded.

But the silence stretched longer than it should have.

"I think we need to take a step back," I said finally.

The words came out quieter than I expected.

But they landed.

Caleb's expression shifted.

Not hurt.

Not yet.

Just trying to understand.

"What do you mean?" he asked.

I exhaled slowly.

"I mean... this," I said, gesturing between us. "It can't go anywhere."

He frowned slightly. "We're not even really—"

"I know," I cut in gently.

And that was the hardest part.

Because he wasn't wrong.

We weren't anything serious.

Just easy.

Comfortable.

Safe.

"I care about you," I said.

And I meant it.

"But that's exactly why I can't do this."

His eyes searched my face.

"This isn't about me, is it?" he asked quietly.

I shook my head.

"No."

A pause.

Then:

"Is it him?"

My chest tightened.

I didn't answer.

I didn't need to.

Caleb let out a slow breath, looking down for a second before nodding.

"Yeah," he said quietly. "I figured."

Guilt hit harder than I expected.

"I'm not—" I started.

"Hey," he cut in gently.

And that was the thing about him.

He was always gentle.

"You don't have to explain it to me," he said.

But I wanted to.

"I just..." I swallowed. "I'm not in a place where I can be anything for anyone right now."

The words felt more true than anything I had said in weeks.

"I thought maybe I could be," I added. "But I can't."

Caleb nodded slowly.

"I get it," he said.

And somehow, that made it worse.

"It's not fair to you," I said.

He gave a small, almost sad smile.

"You don't get to decide what's fair for me."

My chest tightened.

"I know," I said softly.

"But I can decide what I can handle."

Silence settled between us.

"I don't want anything to happen to you because of me," I added quietly.

That made him look up.

"What does that mean?"

I shook my head.

"It just means... I need space."

He studied me for a second longer.

Then finally, he nodded.

"Okay."

No argument.

No pushback.

Just acceptance.

And somehow, that hurt more than anything else.

He didn't stay long after that.

A quick goodbye.

No hug this time.

Just distance.

Like we both understood what this was.

I sat there for a while after he left.

The quiet settling in around me again.

But this time, it didn't feel as heavy.

It felt clearer.

Like I had finally made a choice that was mine.

My phone buzzed.

Stephen.

I didn't look at it.

Didn't pick it up.

Didn't let myself think about what it said.

Because I already knew.

And for the first time, that didn't matter.

Two days later, I packed the last of my things.

The apartment looked empty now.

Bare.

Like nothing had ever happened there.

But I knew better.

I always would.

Bella sat by the door, watching me quietly.

"Ready?" Mallory asked from behind me.

I nodded.

And for the first time in a long time, it felt real.

Not easy.

Not fixed.

But different.

I grabbed my keys.

Took one last look around.

Then stepped out.

And didn't look back.

EIGHT
NEW KEYS

The apartment smelled different.

That was the first thing I noticed.

Not stale.

Not heavy.

Just new.

Fresh paint.

Clean floors.

Windows open just enough to let the air move through.

Nothing in it yet.

No furniture.

No memories.

No him.

I stood just inside the doorway, keys still in my hand.

"Okay," Mallory said behind me, stepping in with a box balanced on her hip. "This is already an upgrade."

I let out a small breath.

Almost a laugh.

"Yeah," I said.

And it felt strange.

Because for the first time in a while, something actually did feel better.

Mallory set the box down in the middle of the living room and looked around like she was already planning everything.

"Couch goes here," she said, pointing. "TV there. We need a rug. Something neutral. Not ugly."

I smiled.

Mallory had always been like this.

Practical.

Straightforward.

The kind of person who just handled things.

We had known each other since school.

Not inseparable.

Not like Lexie.

But steady.

She had seen enough.

Been around enough.

She knew what things looked like with Stephen. Didn't need the full story to understand it wasn't right.

And still, she showed up.

"Hey," she said, glancing at me. "You okay?"

I nodded.

"Yeah."

This time, it didn't feel like a lie.

We spent the next few hours unpacking.

Boxes opened.

Things placed wherever they fit for now.

No pressure to make it perfect.

Just livable.

Mallory turned on music at some point.

Not loud.

Just enough to fill the space.

And for a while, I didn't feel like I was waiting for something to go wrong.

Bella explored everything like it was hers already.

Sniffing corners.

Circling the living room.

Eventually settling near the window where the light hit just right.

"You like this place, huh?" I murmured.

She didn't answer.

But she didn't look tense.

And somehow, that mattered more than anything.

"Okay," Mallory said, stepping back and looking around. "This is a solid first day."

I followed her gaze.

The place wasn't finished.

Not even close.

But it didn't feel empty.

It felt open.

Like something could actually start here.

I walked into my room slowly.

Smaller than the last one.

Simpler.

Just a bed frame for now.

A dresser.

A box still half-unpacked in the corner.

But it didn't feel wrong.

I sat down on the edge of the bed, my fingers brushing over the comforter absently.

No marks.

No damage.

No memories I couldn't escape.

Just quiet.

And for the first time in a long time, quiet didn't feel dangerous.

It just felt unfamiliar.

My phone buzzed.

My chest tightened automatically.

That reaction still lived in me.

I picked it up slowly.

Unknown number.

I exhaled.

Not him.

Not this time.

Still, I set the phone back down.

Not ready to fully relax.

Not yet.

Mallory leaned against the doorframe.

"You know," she said, "this is a really good thing."

I looked up at her.

"It doesn't feel real yet."

She nodded.

"It won't for a while."

A pause.

"But it will."

I let that sit.

Didn't argue it.

Didn't fully believe it either.

Just held onto it.

That night, we sat on the floor in the living room.

Takeout containers spread out between us.

Boxes still stacked around the walls.

Bella curled up nearby.

"This is kind of nice," Mallory said.

"It is," I admitted.

And it was.

Simple.

No tension.

No second-guessing.

No feeling like I had to read the room before I spoke.

Just normal.

Or something close to it.

Later, when everything settled, I lay in bed staring at the ceiling.

The room dark.

The air still.

Different.

Not better.

Not fixed.

But different.

And right now, that was enough.

I turned onto my side, pulling the blanket closer.

Letting myself sit in the quiet a little longer.

Because even though part of me still felt tangled up in everything I had left behind, there was another part of me that knew this was the beginning of something else.

Something I hadn't felt in a long time.

Something I wasn't sure I trusted yet.

But something I wasn't ready to run from either.

NINE

HOLDING THE LINE

The messages didn't stop.

They came in waves.

I miss you.

You know this isn't over.

You can't just ignore me.

Anna, please.

Talk to me.

At first, my chest tightened every time my phone lit up.

That same pull.

That same instinct to answer.

But this time, I didn't.

I let them sit.

Unread.

Unanswered.

And the longer I did, the easier it got.

Not easy.

Just possible.

By the end of the week, I had stopped checking as much.

Stopped letting it control the way my day moved.

Work helped.

The massage place was quiet that night.

The kind of slow shift that made time drag just enough.

By the time I locked up, the parking lot was mostly empty.

Dark.

Still.

I stepped outside, pulling my jacket tighter around me as I reached into my bag for my keys.

And that's when I saw him.

Stephen.

Standing near the edge of the lot.

My stomach dropped.

Not sharp like before.

Just heavy.

Like something I had been expecting, even if I didn't want to admit it.

"What are you doing here?" I asked, my voice tighter than I meant it to be.

"I just wanted to talk," he said.

His tone was calm.

Too calm.

"You can't just show up like this," I said.

"I'm not doing anything," he replied, stepping a little closer. "I'm just standing here."

My grip tightened around my keys.

"You need to leave."

"Why?" he asked.

Like he didn't know.

Like none of this was real.

"Because I'm asking you to," I said.

A pause.

Then:

"You didn't seem to have a problem with me being around you before," he said.

My chest tightened instantly.

"When you let me in."

The words hit harder than anything else.

Like everything that had happened was suddenly being turned back on me.

"That doesn't matter," I said quickly. "You need to go."

"It matters to me."

His voice stayed low.

Controlled.

"I'm serious," I said, my voice shaking now despite myself. "You need to leave before I call someone."

A pause.

Then a small, almost dismissive exhale.

"You really going to do that?" he asked.

"Yes."

The word came out faster this time.

Stronger.

Because I meant it.

And maybe he heard that.

Because after a second, he stopped moving.

Just stood there.

Watching me.

I didn't wait.

I turned, walking quickly to my car, my hands shaking slightly as I unlocked it.

I could feel him still there.

Watching.

I got in.

Locked the door immediately.

And for a second, I just sat there.

Breathing.

Trying to steady my hands enough to start the car.

When I finally pulled out, I didn't look back.

My phone was in my hand before I even made it out of the lot.

Mom.

She answered on the second ring.

"Hey, what's wrong?"

I swallowed.

"He was here," I said.

A pause.

"Where?"

"Work. Just now. In the parking lot."

Silence.

Then:

"I'll handle it."

Her voice wasn't soft anymore.

It was firm.

Certain.

And for the first time in a while, I didn't feel like I had to figure it out on my own.

The next night, there was a squad car parked outside when I locked up.

I stopped when I saw it.

The officer stepped out, giving me a small nod.

"Anna?" he asked.

I nodded.

"Just making sure you get to your car okay," he said.

My chest tightened.

But this time, it wasn't fear.

It was something else.

Relief.

It went on like that for a few days.

Not every night.

But enough.

Enough that I stopped looking over my shoulder as much.

Enough that the walk to my car didn't feel like something I had to prepare for.

Enough that I could breathe a little easier.

By the end of the week, things felt different.

Not fixed.

But steadier.

The apartment was almost fully put together now.

Boxes gone.

Furniture in place.

It actually looked like somewhere people lived.

"Okay," Mallory said, standing in the middle of the living room with her hands on her hips. "We need to have people over."

I laughed.

"For what?"

"For existing," she said. "For surviving. For this not being depressing."

I smiled.

She wasn't wrong.

"It's too early for St. Patrick's Day," I said.

"And too late for Valentine's," she added.

A pause.

Then:

"Saint Practice Day," she said.

I laughed.

"That's terrible."

"It's perfect," she shot back.

And for the first time in a while, it felt like something to look forward to.

Not a distraction.

Not something to avoid thinking about.

Just something good.

I looked around the apartment.

At the space we had built.

At the life that was slowly starting to feel like mine again.

And for the first time, I realized something.

I hadn't answered him.

Not once.

And I wasn't going to.

TEN
SAINT PRACTICE DAY

By the time Saturday rolled around, the apartment didn't feel new anymore.

It felt lived in.

Not perfect.

Not finished.

But ours.

Music played low from Mallory's speaker as she moved around the kitchen, pouring drinks into plastic cups like she had done it a hundred times before.

"Okay," she said, glancing at me. "We're calling this a success already."

I laughed.

"People aren't even here yet."

"Exactly," she said. "That's the best part."

By the time the first knock came, the energy had already shifted.

Not heavy.

Not quiet.

Light.

People trickled in slowly.

Friends.

Old faces.

And new ones too — people I didn't recognize, filtering in behind Mallory's friends like they had always been part of this.

Music got louder.

Voices layered over each other.

Someone set up beer pong in the kitchen, cups lining the counter as people crowded around, cheering louder than necessary.

"Alright, who's playing?" someone yelled.

"Not me," I laughed, stepping out of the way.

The apartment filled quickly.

And for once, it didn't feel overwhelming.

It felt alive.

At some point, I ended up in my room with the door half-closed.

The music muffled just enough.

A few old friends sat around — people I hadn't seen in a while.

The kind of familiar that didn't need catching up right away.

We passed the hookah between us, the air hazy, laughter softer in here.

"You've been MIA," one of them said, nudging me lightly.

"I know," I said, exhaling slowly.

"You're back now?"

I hesitated.

"Trying to be."

They nodded.

No pressure.

Just understanding.

And for a little while, I stayed there.

Talking.

Laughing.

Letting myself feel normal.

By the time I stood up, I was already a little tipsy.

Just enough to feel it.

Light.

I pushed the door open and stepped back into the hallway.

The music hit me first.

Then the voices.

Then the energy.

And that's when I saw him.

Right as I stepped out.

He was walking in through the front door with one of Mallory's friends.

Tall.

Dark hair.

And for a second, everything else blurred.

His smile was the first thing I noticed.

Easy.

Effortless.

The kind of smile that didn't need to try.

But it was his eyes that caught me.

Green.

Stronger than I expected.

There was something in them.

Not intense.

Not overwhelming.

Just steady.

And the way he looked at me wasn't like anyone else had.

There was something almost innocent in it.

Like he was seeing me without everything else attached.

Like I wasn't complicated.

Like I wasn't broken.

My chest tightened.

Because I didn't recognize that feeling.

Not anymore.

Who was he?

The thought came without hesitation.

Clear.

Immediate.

I had to know.

I had to meet him.

Across the room, Lexie caught my eye.

She followed my gaze.

Then looked back at me.

A slow smile spread across her face.

I shook my head immediately.

She didn't believe me.

Not for a second.

I took a step forward.

Then another.

The noise around me faded just slightly.

Because for some reason, I was focused on him.

And I didn't even know why yet.

ELEVEN
SOMETHING DIFFERENT

People moved around me.

Music louder now.

Voices overlapping.

But I wasn't paying attention to any of it.

Because he was still there.

Talking to someone near the door.

Mallory caught me just before I got there.

"Anna," she said, grabbing my arm lightly. "Perfect timing."

She turned, motioning toward them.

"This is Vinny," she said. "We had classes together."

I smiled politely. "Hey."

Vinny nodded, mid-conversation — but I barely registered him.

Because Mallory kept going.

"And this—" she said, glancing over, "—is Wes. He came with Vinny."

My eyes lifted to his.

Up close, it was worse.

Or better.

I wasn't sure.

"Hey," he said.

Simple.

But the way he said it — like he already knew me somehow — made my chest tighten.

"Hi," I said.

My voice softer than I meant it to be.

Mallory was already moving.

"Come on," she said. "They need more people for beer pong."

We made our way into the kitchen, squeezing past people gathered around the counter.

"Alright, we've got next," someone called out.

"There's no chairs," Vinny said, looking around.

"Figure it out," Mallory shot back.

I laughed, glancing down before spotting a laundry basket flipped upside down near the wall.

"Perfect," I said.

I moved to sit.

And the second I put my weight on it, it collapsed.

The plastic caved in instantly, the basket folding as I dropped straight through.

Laughter erupted around me.

"Oh my—" someone started.

I covered my face, laughing as I tried to pull myself out.

"Okay, that was not my fault."

A hand reached down toward me.

Wes.

"Here," he said, smiling.

I took it.

And the second he pulled me up, everything else faded.

Just for a second.

His hand was warm.

Steady.

And when I looked up, his eyes were right there.

Green.

Softer now.

Closer.

And the way he looked at me — it didn't feel like anything I had felt before.

Not intense.

Not overwhelming.

Just real.

"Strong choice on the chair," he said.

I laughed, shaking my head. "Clearly."

We ended up standing off to the side instead of playing.

Talking.

The game faded into the background.

At some point, we drifted out of the kitchen, the noise getting louder behind us as we moved toward the living room.

It felt quieter there.

Or maybe I just noticed him more.

We sat down on the couch.

Bella immediately climbed up beside us, tail wagging like she had decided he was hers now.

"Well, I think I've been replaced," I said.

Wes laughed, reaching down to pet her. "She seems like she has good taste."

"Debatable," I said.

He grabbed a chip from the bowl on the table, holding it out. "Alright," he said seriously, "I'm going to teach her how to shake."

I laughed. "She already knows how to shake."

Bella sat up instantly, paw already lifting slightly as she stared at the chip.

Wes paused, looking between her and me. "Okay, but she looks like she's learning it for the first time."

"That's because she'll do anything for food."

"Same," he said.

I laughed again.

And this time, it felt natural.

Not forced.

Not something I had to think about.

Bella took the chip, wagging her tail harder as Wes scratched behind her ears.

"She's my new favorite," he said.

"She says that about everyone with snacks," I replied.

"Good. I respect that."

The conversation didn't stop.

Didn't stall.

Stories.

Jokes.

Little things that didn't matter.

But somehow, it all did.

Because for the first time in a long time, I wasn't thinking about what I should say.

Or how I should act.

Or what something meant.

I was just there.

With him.

And the way he looked at me — it didn't feel like he was trying to figure me out.

Or control anything.

It felt like he was just seeing me.

Exactly as I was.

And for some reason, that felt unfamiliar.

In the best way.

TWELVE
NOT WHAT I EXPECTED

The party didn't end all at once.

It faded.

Music lower.

Voices softer.

People scattered between rooms — some still playing, some just sitting around like they didn't want it to be over yet.

Beer pong cups still lined the counter.

Someone arguing over rules that didn't matter anymore.

I barely noticed.

Because I was still thinking about him.

Wes.

Every time I looked up, I found him again.

Across the room.

Talking.

Laughing.

And somehow, still looking at me like he had earlier.

Like I was the only thing in the room that hadn't changed.

I hadn't even noticed who else was there.

Not really.

Miles had been around.

In and out of conversations.

Easy.

Familiar.

But not important.

Not like before.

David came and went too.

That felt different now.

We weren't as close.

After everything — after Stephen — things had shifted.

Not because of something anyone said.

Just distance.

It was easier not to be around that crowd.

Too many memories.

Too many things I didn't want to feel again.

By the time the night started to wind down, people were crashing wherever they could.

The couch.

The floor.

Anywhere open.

Wes and his friends didn't leave.

They stayed.

Responsible.

Like they weren't trying to push the night further than it needed to go.

And I noticed that.

Even if I didn't say it out loud.

Eventually, I slipped into my room.

The noise outside dulling just enough as I closed the door behind me.

I exhaled.

The night catching up all at once.

A soft knock came a second later.

Miles.

I didn't think twice.

"Come in."

He stepped inside like he had a hundred times before.

Familiar.

Comfortable.

"Long night," he said.

"Yeah."

We talked for a bit.

Nothing serious.

Nothing heavy.

Just easy.

The kind of conversation that didn't ask anything from me.

At some point, he stretched out on the floor, grabbing a pillow from the corner.

"You good if I crash here?" he asked.

"Yeah," I said.

And I meant it.

Because there was nothing there.

Not anymore.

Just history.

Friendship.

Safe, in a way that didn't confuse me.

I climbed into bed, staring up at the ceiling.

My mind drifting back to him.

Wes.

The way he looked at me.

The way it felt.

Different.

And somewhere in the back of my mind, a thought slipped in.

What did that look like?

To him?

The noise.

The people.

Miles in my room.

I frowned slightly.

I hadn't even thought about it.

Not once.

Because for the first time, I wasn't thinking about what something meant.

I was just living it.

THIRTEEN

I HAD TO KNOW

A couple days later, it was almost the weekend again.

Mallory's phone buzzed from across the room.

"Vinny," she said, glancing at the screen. "It's his birthday this weekend."

I looked up. "Oh."

"They're all going out," she added. "Some bar downtown."

A pause.

My chest tightened slightly.

I tried to play it off. "Cool."

Mallory looked at me.

She knew.

She always knew just enough.

"You want me to ask if he's going?" she said casually.

I hesitated.

Then nodded.

"Yeah."

She typed quickly.

Waited.

Then:

"He'll be there," she said, looking back at me.

That was it.

That was all I needed.

"We're going," I said.

No hesitation.

Later, I stood in front of the mirror.

The room quiet.

The air still.

I stared at myself longer than I meant to.

My hair fell just above my shoulders now.

Shorter.

Darker.

Different.

And tucked underneath — barely noticeable unless you were looking for them — were a few peek-a-boo streaks of purple.

I reached up, pulling a section forward, letting the color catch the light.

It wasn't something I would've done before.

But that felt like the point.

I had changed it because I needed to.

Needed something that felt like mine.

Something I chose.

Something no one else had touched.

I let the strand fall back into place slowly.

Trying to decide if I liked it.

Trying to decide if I liked me.

I was shorter than most girls.

Always had been.

And there were still moments — like this — where I noticed everything I didn't love first.

But I wasn't the same.

Not completely.

And I could see that now.

Even if I didn't fully understand it yet.

Even if I didn't fully believe it.

Mallory leaned against the doorframe behind me.

"You've been staring at yourself for like five minutes," she said.

"I'm thinking."

"Dangerous," she replied.

I smiled slightly.

Mallory was easy in a different way than Lexie.

Less emotional.

More real.

The kind of person who didn't overcomplicate things.

"Relax," she said. "You look hot."

I laughed. "Shut up."

"I'm serious," she said. "That hair? It works."

I looked back at myself.

Maybe it did.

My phone sat on the dresser.

Quiet.

For the first time in weeks — completely quiet.

I had changed my number.

Finally.

It had been the only way.

The only way to make it stop.

The messages.

The calls.

The constant pull.

Gone.

Just like that.

And even though part of me still felt it, the space it left behind felt cleaner.

I picked up my jacket.

My heart starting to pick up slightly.

Not fear.

Something else.

Nerves.

Anticipation.

Confusion.

Because I didn't know what this was yet.

Didn't know what he was.

Didn't know if I was ready.

But I knew one thing.

I wanted to find out.

"I'm not ready for anything serious," I said quietly.

Mallory shrugged.

"Good," she said. "Then don't make it serious."

I let that sit.

Didn't overthink it.

For once.

"Come on," she said, grabbing her bag. "Let's go."

And just like that, I stepped out of the apartment.

Into something new.

Even if I didn't know what it was yet.

FOURTEEN
GREEN EYES

The bar was loud.

Music too high.

Voices layered over each other.

Glasses clinking somewhere behind the chaos.

The air thick.

Warm.

Crowded.

The kind of place that used to make my chest tighten.

But not tonight.

Because the second I saw him, everything else blurred.

Wes.

Standing near the bar, talking to Vinny.

And just like before, my pulse quickened.

Not in that sharp, anxious way I had gotten used to.

Something softer.

Pulling.

He looked up.

And when his eyes met mine, there it was again.

Green.

But not just green.

Steady.

Like he wasn't searching for something in me.

Like he wasn't trying to figure me out.

Like he was just seeing me.

"Hey," he said when I got close.

Simple.

But it felt like more.

"Hi," I said.

And suddenly, the noise around us faded.

Not completely.

Just enough.

We ended up at the bar first.

Drinks in hand.

Mallory somewhere behind me, talking to Vinny and the rest of Wes's friends — some of which I hadn't met yet.

But I barely noticed.

Because once we started talking, it didn't stop.

Movies.

That's what it started with.

"I'm telling you, it's one of the best movies ever made," he said.

"You say that about every movie," I laughed.

"Not true," he said. "Just the good ones."

"Which are... all of them?"

"Exactly."

I shook my head, smiling. "You're impossible."

"And yet," he said lightly, "you're still talking to me."

I laughed again.

And it felt easy.

Too easy.

We talked about everything.

Movies turned into favorite scenes.

Favorite scenes turned into stories.

Stories turned into nothing and everything at the same time.

And somehow, hours passed.

Without me checking the time.

Without me checking my phone.

Without me thinking about anything else.

At one point, he leaned slightly against the bar, looking at me a little differently.

More focused.

"I didn't think you were interested," he said.

I blinked. "What?"

"That night," he added. "At your place."

My chest tightened slightly.

"Oh," I said, shaking my head. "No — Miles just... he's a friend."

Wes nodded slowly. "Yeah?"

"Yeah," I said. "There's nothing there."

And for the first time, I meant it without hesitation.

He held my gaze for a second longer.

Like he was deciding whether to believe me.

Then he smiled.

"Good," he said.

The word landed softly.

But it stayed.

Another drink.

Another conversation.

Another hour I didn't notice passing.

"You ever actually go on dates?" he asked at one point.

I laughed slightly. "Not really."

He raised an eyebrow. "Not really?"

"Not like... real ones," I said.

And suddenly, I realized how true that was.

Bars.

Houses.

Parties.

But never this.

Never something that felt like it had intention.

Wes nodded slowly.

"Alright," he said.

A pause.

Then:

"Let me take you on one."

My heart skipped.

"Like... a real date?" I asked.

"Yeah," he said simply. "Sunday."

I hesitated.

Not because I didn't want to.

Because I did.

Too much.

And that scared me.

"Okay," I said.

And just like that, something shifted.

Later, we stood outside.

The air cooler now.

Quieter than inside.

Mallory was already calling the Uber.

I turned back toward him.

"Text me," he said, holding out his phone.

I took it, typing in my number.

A small pause.

Then handed it back.

"Sunday," he said again.

"Sunday," I repeated.

For a second, neither of us moved.

Like neither of us wanted to break whatever this was.

Then Mallory called my name.

"Uber's here."

I nodded, stepping back. "Bye."

"Bye," he said.

I got into the car.

The door closing softly behind me.

And for a second, I just sat there.

My chest full.

Not heavy.

Just full.

Mallory glanced over at me. "Well?" she said.

I shook my head slightly. "I don't know."

But I did.

It felt different.

Too different.

As the car pulled away, I looked out the window.

Watching him get smaller in the distance.

Until he was gone.

My phone stayed quiet in my lap.

And that's when I noticed it.

The silence.

No messages.

No missed calls.

Nothing.

Because part of me — the part that hadn't caught up yet — was waiting for it.

Waiting for something to go wrong.

For the other shoe to drop.

Because things like this didn't just happen.

Not to me.

Not anymore.

I leaned back in the seat, exhaling slowly.

Trying to hold onto the feeling.

The lightness.

The ease.

Even with that quiet worry sitting underneath it.

Because for the first time, I wasn't just scared.

I was hopeful.

And I didn't know what to do with that yet.

FIFTEEN
HOW DO I DO THIS?

The next morning felt different.

Not heavy.

Not quiet in that suffocating way.

Just slow.

I lay in bed for a while, staring at the ceiling.

Thinking about him.

Wes.

The way he looked at me.

The way it felt — easy.

Too easy.

My pulse quickened slightly.

Because part of me still didn't trust it.

By that night, the apartment was quieter.

No music.

No crowd.

Just me, Mallory — and Lexie.

Of course Lexie came over.

She always did.

She sat curled up on the couch, legs tucked under her like she lived there too.

"Alright," she said, pointing at me. "Start talking."

Mallory laughed from the kitchen.

"Yes," she called out. "I want details."

I rolled my eyes slightly. "It wasn't like that."

"It's always like that," Lexie said.

I smiled despite myself.

And then I told them.

Everything.

The bar.

The conversation.

The way it didn't feel forced.

"The way he looks at you?" Mallory added, walking in with a drink.

I paused. "Yeah."

Lexie tilted her head slightly. "How?"

I hesitated.

"I don't know," I said. "Just different."

They exchanged a look.

"Different good?" Mallory asked.

I nodded slowly. "Yeah."

A pause.

Then:

"I think he's going to ask me out again."

Lexie smiled.

"I think he already did."

"Sunday," I said.

Mallory's eyes widened slightly. "A real date?"

I laughed. "I think so."

Lexie leaned back into the couch, watching me carefully.

"And how do you feel about that?"

I hesitated.

"Excited," I admitted.

Then: "Terrified."

They both nodded.

"Good," Mallory said.

I blinked. "What?"

"That means it matters," she said.

Lexie shook her head slightly. "That means she's overthinking it."

"Also true," Mallory added.

I laughed.

And for a second, it felt normal.

My phone buzzed on the counter.

Mallory grabbed it. "Matt," she said.

I sat up slightly. "Answer it."

"Hey," I said, leaning against the counter.

"Hey, you alive?" he asked.

I smiled. "Barely."

"Yeah, I heard you've been busy," he said.

There was something underneath it.

Checking.

Always checking.

"I'm good," I said.

"Yeah?"

"Yeah."

A pause.

Then:

"I'm heading to Chicago this weekend," he said. "St. Patty's with the guys."

"Of course you are," I laughed.

"But," he added, "I told Mom I'd stop by on my way back."

My chest softened slightly. "Yeah?"

"Yeah," he said. "I want to see the new place. Take you out to dinner before I head back to school."

"I'd like that."

Mallory walked in, grabbing a drink. "Who's that?" she mouthed.

"My brother," I said, putting him on speaker.

"Hey," she said.

"Hey," Matt replied.

A small pause.

Something subtle.

"So you're the roommate," he said.

"That's me," she smiled. "I'm making sure your sister survives."

"I appreciate that," he said.

"I do too," I added.

Mallory smirked slightly.

"We'll be here Monday," she said. "If you're still planning dinner."

"I am," he said. "Don't let her cancel."

"I won't."

"I'm right here," I said.

"Good," Matt replied. "Then I'll see you."

The call ended.

Mallory looked at me. "Well."

"What?" I asked.

She shook her head. "Nothing."

But her smile said everything.

The next day — Sunday.

I stood in front of the mirror.

Staring.

"I don't know what to wear."

Mallory walked straight into the room. "Good thing you have me."

We ended up in her closet.

Clothes everywhere.

"Too much?" she asked, holding something up.

"Yes."

"Too boring?"

"Yes."

She sighed. "You're impossible."

"I'm nervous."

She stopped.

Looked at me.

"That's okay," she said.

I swallowed.

"I don't know how to do this."

She stepped a little closer.

"I know," she said. "But you don't have to."

A pause.

"Just go."

I nodded slowly.

Because she was right.

I didn't have to know everything.

I didn't have to get it perfect.

I just had to show up.

And for the first time in a long time, that didn't feel impossible.

It just felt new.

SIXTEEN
EASY

He was on time.

That was the first thing I noticed.

Not early.

Not late.

Just there.

I glanced out the window when I saw headlights pull up.

A white G6.

My pulse quickened slightly.

I grabbed my jacket, glancing at myself one more time in the mirror before heading out.

Mallory's voice followed behind me. "You look hot. Go."

I laughed under my breath. "Stop."

But I didn't argue.

The air was cooler outside.

I walked toward the car, my heart beating just a little faster than I wanted it to.

He stepped out when he saw me.

Not leaning against the car.

Not waiting.

He got out.

"Hey," he said, smiling.

And there it was again.

That feeling.

"Hi."

He opened the door for me.

Simple.

But it caught me off guard.

"Thank you," I said.

"Of course."

The drive was effortless.

Music low.

Conversation soft.

No pressure.

No awkward silence.

Just comfortable.

"So," he said, glancing over at me, "movie first or dinner first?"

"Movie," I said.

"Good," he smiled. "That's what I was thinking."

The theater was busy.

People everywhere.

But somehow, it didn't feel overwhelming.

Not with him next to me.

We got our tickets.

Divergent.

"Have you seen it?" he asked.

"No."

"You'll like it," he said. "Trust me."

I smiled slightly.

Trust me.

The words lingered longer than they should have.

Inside, the lights dimmed.

We sat side by side.

Just close enough to feel it.

Not touching.

Not pushing anything.

Just there.

And for once, I didn't feel like I had to read into every little thing.

After the movie, we walked out into the night air.

"Well?" he asked.

"I liked it."

"Told you."

I laughed.

Dinner was Max & Erma's.

Casual.

Simple.

But it felt intentional.

Like he had thought about it.

Like this wasn't just something to do.

It was something he wanted to do.

He held the door again.

Pulled my chair out.

Little things.

But they stacked.

And the more they did, the more something inside me didn't know what to do with it.

"You're really nice," I said at one point.

The words slipped out before I could stop them.

He smiled slightly. "Is that a bad thing?"

"No," I said quickly. "Just different."

He nodded. "Different good?"

I hesitated. "Yeah."

But my stomach fluttered anyway.

Because good hadn't always meant safe.

"What about you?" he asked. "Have you always been this hard to read?"

I laughed softly. "I don't think I used to be."

"What changed?"

The question was gentle.

But it landed heavy.

I looked down at my hands for a second.

"I was in something messy," I said finally.

Not a lie.

Not the whole truth either.

His expression didn't change.

Didn't push.

Didn't press for more.

"Messy how?" he asked, softer now.

I shook my head slightly. "Just not what I thought it was."

A pause.

Then: "Okay," he said.

Just that.

No questions.

No judgment.

And somehow, that made my chest tighten even more.

Because I was waiting for it.

The shift.

The reaction.

Something.

But it didn't come.

After dinner, we ended up back at the apartment.

Not planned.

Just natural.

Mallory wasn't home.

The place was quiet.

Calm.

We sat on the couch.

Bella immediately climbed between us like she had been waiting for him.

"Well, I see how it is," I said.

"She's my dog now," he said casually, scratching behind her ears.

"Absolutely not."

"She made her choice."

I laughed.

And again, it felt unforced.

We talked for a while.

About everything.

Nothing.

The kind of conversation that didn't feel like it had an end point.

And the whole time, he didn't push.

Didn't move closer than I was comfortable with.

Didn't try to turn the night into something it didn't need to be.

He just stayed.

Present.

And for the first time, I realized something.

I wasn't waiting for him to change.

I was waiting for something to go wrong.

"You're thinking again," he said quietly.

I smiled slightly. "Is it that obvious?"

"A little."

I exhaled softly. "I'm just not used to this."

"This?" he asked.

I looked at him.

"Something that feels easy."

He held my gaze for a second.

Then: "It's supposed to feel that way," he said.

My chest tightened again.

Because I didn't know if I believed that.

Later, he stood by the door.

"Text me when you get back in," he said.

I smiled slightly. "I'm already here."

He laughed. "Then text me anyway."

I walked him out.

Watched as he got into his car.

The white G6 pulling away slowly.

And for a second, I just stood there.

Taking it in.

The quiet.

The calm.

The way the night had felt.

Different.

Too different.

Because part of me still didn't trust it.

Still didn't trust that something this easy would actually stay.

I closed the door behind me.

Leaning back against it for a second.

Bella settling at my feet.

And even though my chest wasn't tight the way it used to be, there was still something there.

A small, quiet voice.

Waiting.

For the other shoe to fall.

SEVENTEEN
I DIDN'T TRUST IT

Time passed differently with him.

Not fast.

Not slow.

Just steady.

A few more dates.

Coffee that turned into hours.

Late nights at the apartment that didn't feel heavy.

Conversations that didn't need effort.

We were spending what felt like every day together.

And every time, I waited.

For something to change.

For him to pull away.

For something to feel off.

For the moment it stopped feeling effortless.

But it didn't.

And that was the problem.

"You're thinking again."

His voice pulled me back.

We were on the couch.

Bella curled up at our feet.

The room quiet in that soft, comfortable way I still didn't fully trust.

"I know," I said.

He smiled slightly. "You always do that when things get quiet."

I looked down at my hands. "I'm not used to quiet."

"I know," he said.

And the way he said it — like he actually meant it — made something in my chest shift.

But it didn't settle.

Because there was still something there.

Something I hadn't told him.

Something I couldn't keep avoiding.

"My life isn't normal," I said finally.

He didn't react.

Just waited.

"I was in a relationship," I continued.

A pause.

"It wasn't good."

That felt like the smallest way to say something that had taken everything out of me.

His expression softened slightly. "Okay," he said.

Just that.

And somehow, that made it harder.

"There's a court date coming up," I added.

That got his attention.

"For what?"

I swallowed. "He violated a restraining order."

The words felt heavy.

Real in a way I couldn't soften.

Wes didn't interrupt.

Didn't rush to respond.

He just listened.

And that terrified me more than anything.

Because now he knew enough to leave.

"I didn't tell you because I thought—" I stopped.

"Thought what?" he asked gently.

I swallowed. "That you wouldn't want this."

The words felt too small.

Too simple for something that had been sitting in my chest for weeks.

"That once you knew, you'd realize I come with too much."

My fingers twisted together in my lap.

A quiet, hollow laugh echoed somewhere inside me.

Miles didn't pick me.

He never did.

Not when it mattered.

And Stephen didn't love me.

Not the way people are supposed to.

Not the way I kept trying to convince myself he did.

He just kept me.

I exhaled slowly, my eyes fixed on my hands.

And I stayed.

Because I thought that was the same thing.

My throat tightened.

Because maybe that's what I am.

Something people want for a while.

Something they hold onto but don't choose.

I shook my head slightly, like I could clear it.

"I just want someone to choose me," I said.

The words hung there.

Too real.

Too exposed.

For a second, I wished I could take them back.

The room went quiet.

Not awkward.

Just still.

I didn't look at him.

I couldn't.

Because I was already bracing for it.

The shift.

The hesitation.

The moment he realized I wasn't simple.

That I wasn't easy.

That I came with too much.

But it didn't come.

Instead, I felt it.

His hand.

Slowly, carefully, resting over mine.

Not grabbing.

Not pulling.

Just there.

Warm.

Steady.

Like he was giving me space — even while he stayed.

My fingers stilled under his.

And for a second, I didn't move.

"You don't have to explain everything right now," he said quietly.

His voice wasn't rushed.

Wasn't trying to fix anything.

It just met me where I was.

I finally looked up.

His eyes were steady.

Not searching.

Not questioning.

Just there.

"I'm not going anywhere. Not tonight," he added.

The words were simple.

But they landed.

Because they weren't big.

They weren't promises.

They were just true.

His thumb brushed lightly against my hand.

Slow.

Grounding.

Like he was trying to keep me here — not pull me anywhere I wasn't ready to go.

"I can tell this wasn't easy for you," he said.

My breath caught.

"And you don't have to figure it all out at once."

A pause.

"You don't have to prove anything to me."

That one hit.

Because I didn't even realize how much I had been trying to.

My grip tightened in his hand without thinking.

And this time, he didn't shift it.

Didn't turn it into something more.

He just held it.

Letting me feel it.

Letting me decide what it meant.

"Let me come with you," he said after a moment.

I blinked. "To court."

The word sat between us.

Heavy.

"You don't have to do that," I said.

"I know."

A small pause.

"But I'd rather you not go through that alone."

My stomach fluttered.

Something softer.

Something unfamiliar.

And even with his hand in mine — even with the way he was looking at me — there was still a part of me that didn't fully believe it.

Didn't know how to.

Because this kind of steady was something I had never been given before.

And I didn't know how long it could last.

Later that night, we ended up outside with friends.

Leaving the bar together.

The air colder now.

Carrying that early hint of spring.

St. Patrick's Day.

People still out somewhere.

Laughter in the distance.

But here, it was quiet.

We stood there for a second.

Neither of us moving.

Like we both felt it.

That shift.

He stepped closer first.

Slow.

Giving me time to move away.

I didn't.

Because for once, I didn't want to run.

His hand brushed mine again.

Then gently, he pulled me closer.

And when he kissed me — it wasn't rushed.

Wasn't overwhelming.

Wasn't something I felt like I had to give into.

It was soft.

Intentional.

Like he was asking — not taking.

And for the first time, I didn't feel like I was losing myself in it.

I felt like I was still there.

When we pulled apart, I exhaled slowly.

My chest full.

Not heavy.

Just full.

"See?" he said quietly.

I smiled slightly. "See what?"

"That not everything has to feel the way it used to."

My breath caught again.

Because I wanted to believe him.

So badly.

But even as I stood there, a small part of me still whispered — this won't last.

The court date sat in the back of my mind.

Heavy.

Waiting.

Like something that would change everything.

Like something that would remind me that this — whatever this was — might not survive it.

Because who would choose someone like me once they knew everything?

I looked at him again.

Standing there.

Still.

Certain.

And for the first time, I let myself wonder:

What if he does?

EIGHTEEN

THE COURT DATE

A couple weeks passed.

Not quietly.

Not completely easy.

But steady.

Wes stayed.

Not in a way that felt overwhelming.

Not in a way that asked anything from me.

He just showed up.

And somehow, that felt harder to understand than anything else.

The courthouse felt cold.

Too bright.

Too quiet in all the wrong ways.

My hands were colder than they should've been.

"You okay?" Wes asked beside me.

I nodded. "Yeah."

Not entirely true.

But closer than it would've been before.

We sat there waiting.

Time stretching longer than it should have.

My eyes kept drifting to the door.

Waiting.

For him.

For the moment everything would feel real again.

But he never showed.

He wasn't there.

But what he did still was.

The room shifted when that realization settled.

Not relief.

Not fully.

Just something different.

"They've issued a warrant for his arrest," someone said.

The words landed heavier than I expected.

Final.

Real.

I swallowed.

Because even without him there, everything still came out.

The messages.

The calls.

The way he showed up.

The things I hadn't said out loud before — suddenly weren't mine to hold onto quietly anymore.

They were spoken.

Documented.

Proven.

I didn't look at Wes while it was happening.

I couldn't.

Because this was the part I had been avoiding.

The part I thought would make him leave.

When it was over, I stood up slowly.

My body felt lighter.

But not free.

Not yet.

We walked outside together.

The air hit different.

Cooler.

Sharper.

Real.

For a second, neither of us said anything.

Then I felt it.

His arm.

Wrapping around me.

Not pulling.

Not overwhelming.

Just there.

Steady.

Like he didn't need words.

Like he knew I didn't either.

"I didn't know it was like that," he said quietly.

My breath hitched.

"I know," I said.

A pause.

"I didn't want you to."

He nodded slightly. "I get that."

And he did.

Or at least, he wasn't making me explain it.

His hand found mine again.

Familiar now.

Grounding.

"You don't have to carry that by yourself anymore," he said.

The words were soft.

Not a promise.

Not a fix.

Just an offering.

I swallowed.

Because part of me still felt like I should.

That I deserved to.

But for the first time, I didn't say it out loud.

We stood there for a second longer.

The courthouse behind us.

The past still close enough to feel — but not holding me the same way anymore.

Because even though the damage was still there, the contact was over.

And that mattered.

More than I thought it would.

NINETEEN
NOT WHAT I EXPECTED

Time moved forward.

Quietly.

Without asking.

Weeks turned into months.

And somehow, things stayed good.

Wes and I saw each other often.

Not planned.

Not forced.

Just natural.

We spent nights at the apartment.

Talking.

Laughing.

Bella curled up between us like she belonged to both of us now.

And when things shifted—when we got closer—it never felt rushed.

Never felt like something I had to give.

He never pushed.

Never crossed a line I didn't want to cross.

And that still confused me.

Because I was waiting for it.

That moment where it changed.

But it didn't.

Somewhere in between all of it, Mallory and Matt had fallen into something too.

Easy.

Like it made sense.

Like it had been there longer than anyone realized.

It was nice.

Having my brother around more.

Having something that felt steady on both sides of my life.

Everything felt safe.

And somehow, that made me uneasy.

"You're coming with me," Wes said one night.

I looked up. "Where?"

"A wedding," he said.

I blinked. "What?"

"My friend Duke," he added. "It's in a couple weeks."

My stomach knotted slightly. "A wedding?"

He smiled. "Yeah."

A pause.

"Come as my date."

Something in me flipped.

Not bad.

Just big.

"Okay," I said.

And just like that, it became real.

The next few days were filled with dresses.

Mallory dragging me from store to store.

My mom texting options like it was her job.

"This one," Mallory said, holding something up.

"No."

"Why?"

"I don't know. It's too—something."

"You're impossible."

"I'm nervous."

She paused.

Then softened slightly. "That's allowed."

Later, I stood in front of the mirror again.

The dress hanging just right.

My hair falling around my shoulders—those faint streaks of purple catching the light if you looked close enough.

I stared at myself.

Trying to see what everyone else saw.

My phone buzzed.

Mom.

"When do I get to meet him?" she asked.

I smiled slightly. "Soon."

"He's not even my boyfriend yet."

There was a pause.

Mallory looked at me from across the room.

"He's taking you to a wedding," she said. "That doesn't count as a boyfriend?"

I let out a small laugh. "I don't know."

But the thought stayed.

Longer than it should have.

Why hasn't he asked?

The question came quietly.

Uninvited.

But it stayed.

Does he not want to?

My chest tightened.

Am I not—

I swallowed.

Not enough?

I looked back at myself in the mirror.

The dress.

The hair.

The version of me I was still trying to understand.

Because even with everything going right, there was still a part of me waiting for it not to be enough.

TWENTY
DO I BELONG HERE?

The night before felt heavier than it should have.

We sat in his car for a while after he told me.

"I'm in the wedding," Wes said.

I blinked. "What?"

"I thought I mentioned it," he added.

He didn't.

My heart stuttered.

"So... I'll just meet you there?" I asked.

"Yeah," he said. "I have to be there early."

A pause.

"I'll find you as soon as I can."

I nodded.

But something in me shifted.

This wasn't what I pictured.

Not walking in alone.

Not sitting by myself.

Not being surrounded by people who already belonged.

"I can Uber," I said quickly.

"I can come get you after," he said.

"It's fine," I said.

Too fast.

Too easy.

"Actually," he said, "can you drive my car tomorrow?"

I blinked. "What?"

"So we only have one car there," he explained. "We can Uber home after, or just stay in one of the hotel rooms Duke and them have blocked off."

A pause.

"I'll have to be there early, so it just makes more sense."

I nodded slowly. "Yeah... okay."

It did make sense.

But something in my stomach still knotted.

Because it meant showing up alone.

Walking into all of it — by myself.

The drive back to his place was quieter than before.

Not awkward.

Just full.

He reached over, his hand resting lightly on my thigh.

Grounding.

"You okay?" he asked.

"Yeah."

Not entirely.

When we pulled up, I stayed in the driver's seat.

This time, he didn't move to get out right away.

Instead, he reached for the keys.

Then paused.

"Take it," he said, placing them gently in my hand.

My fingers curled around them automatically.

"You'll be fine," he added softly.

A small smile.

Not pushing.

Just steady.

"I'll find you as soon as I can tomorrow."

I nodded. "I know."

But it wasn't him I was worried about.

It was everything else.

He leaned in slightly, pressing a soft kiss to my lips.

Gentle.

"Tomorrow's going to be okay," he said.

I wanted to believe him.

So badly.

I watched him walk inside.

And then I drove.

The radio clicked on automatically.

And within seconds, *She Will Be Loved* filled the car.

My breath caught.

Of course.

Of all songs — that one.

It's not always rainbows and butterflies...

I swallowed hard.

My hands tightening slightly on the steering wheel.

Because that song always did this.

Made something in me ache in a way I couldn't explain.

I don't mind spending every day...

Tears blurred my vision.

I blinked them away quickly.

But they didn't stop.

Because somewhere deep down, there was still a part of me that didn't believe I was the one someone stayed for.

That didn't believe I was the one someone chose.

And as I drove, that feeling sat heavy in my chest.

Because tomorrow, I was walking into his world.

And I didn't know if I belonged in it.

The church was already filling when I got there.

Rows of people.

Families.

Friends.

Everyone knowing where to go.

Where to sit.

I stood there for a second — frozen.

Before finally slipping into a seat near the back.

Alone.

The ceremony blurred.

Not because I wasn't watching — but because my mind kept drifting.

To him.

Somewhere up there.

Part of something I wasn't in yet.

Afterward, people filtered outside.

Groups forming.

Laughter building.

And I stayed back for a second.

Trying to breathe.

Trying not to let the feeling take over.

"Hey."

I turned.

Wes.

Finally.

Relief hit me before I could stop it.

"Hey," I said.

He stepped closer, his hand brushing mine. "You made it."

I nodded. "Yeah."

He smiled slightly. "I'm glad you're here."

And just like that, something in my chest loosened.

"Come here," he said.

He guided me gently through the crowd.

"This is Duke," he said.

The groom.

Already a little tipsy.

"Finally," Duke laughed, pulling me into a quick hug. "I've heard so much about you."

I smiled awkwardly. "Hopefully good things."

"Only the best," he said.

I wasn't sure I believed that.

The reception was louder.

Music.

Drinks.

Voices louder than before.

And the more I watched, the more something in my stomach knotted.

Because the guys were already drinking.

Louder.

Looser.

And even though I told myself this wasn't the same, my body didn't fully believe it.

I sat at the table quietly.

Wes pulled away again.

Back to his responsibilities.

And suddenly, I was alone again.

"This seat taken?"

I looked up.

Avery.

Beautiful.

Effortless.

The kind of pretty that didn't try — but still felt intimidating.

"Go ahead," I said.

Kyler sat next to her.

Vinny's date across from me.

Familiar faces.

But not mine.

"So," Avery said, looking at me, "you're Anna."

I nodded. "Yeah."

She smiled.

Kind.

But observant.

Like she was trying to figure me out.

Not in a bad way.

Just carefully.

I answered their questions.

Smiled when I was supposed to.

But inside, I felt out of place.

Like I was sitting in someone else's life.

Dinner passed slowly.

Until finally — he came back.

Wes.

Sliding into the seat beside me like he had always been there.

"You good?" he asked quietly.

I nodded. "Yeah."

And this time, it felt a little more true.

After dinner, things shifted.

Music louder.

People moving.

And then — *Mr. Brightside* started playing.

The room erupted.

People singing.

Dancing.

And for a second, I just watched.

Until his hand found mine.

"Come on," he said. "I know this is your favorite song."

I hesitated.

Just for a second.

Then I went.

We moved into the crowd.

The noise.

The chaos.

But somehow, it didn't feel overwhelming.

Not with him.

We danced.

Not perfectly.

Not planned.

Just together.

And for the first time all day, I didn't feel like I was watching it from the outside.

I felt like I was in it.

I looked up at him.

His green eyes finding mine again.

And for a second, everything else disappeared.

And even with the noise — even with the people — it felt quiet.

Just us.

My breath caught.

Not from fear.

Something else.

Something I wasn't used to.

Because for the first time all day, I didn't feel like I didn't belong.

TWENTY-ONE
UNDER THE LIGHTS

The night had softened.

The music still played inside.

Laughter spilled out through the open doors.

But outside, it was quieter.

String lights stretched overhead, casting a warm glow across the patio.

I stepped out for a second.

Just to breathe.

The air cool against my skin, grounding me in a way the room hadn't.

"Hey."

I turned.

Wes.

Of course.

He stepped closer, his hand brushing mine like it always did now.

Familiar.

"You okay?" he asked.

"Yeah," I said.

And this time, it wasn't a lie.

We stood there for a second.

The lights above us swaying slightly in the breeze.

Inside, someone yelled.

Someone laughed.

But out here, everything had slowed down.

"I was talking to Duke earlier," he said.

I nodded.

"He asked if I was bringing my girlfriend."

My pulse quickened.

"And?" I asked.

A small smile pulled at his lips. "I said yeah."

I looked at him.

Really looked at him.

"You did?"

"Yeah," he said, like it was obvious.

A pause.

"Well... you never asked," I said quietly.

The words sat between us.

Not sharp.

Just honest.

His expression shifted.

Not defensive.

Just surprised.

"I didn't?" he asked.

I shook my head.

"I didn't know if that's what this was."

A small silence fell between us.

Then he let out a breath, running a hand through his hair.

"I thought it just was," he said.

I gave a small, almost nervous laugh.

"I didn't know if you wanted it to be."

His brows pulled together slightly.

"I do," he said quickly. "I just—"

He shook his head, a small smile breaking through. "I feel like an idiot."

I smiled a little. "You're not."

"I should've asked you," he said.

And the way he said it—like it mattered—made something in my chest shift warmer.

He stepped a little closer.

The lights catching in his eyes.

Green.

Steady.

"Anna," he said.

Simple.

But it pulled my attention fully to him.

"Will you be my girlfriend?"

It was a little cheesy.

A little awkward.

But it was him.

And somehow, that made it perfect.

My heart stuttered.

"Yes," I said.

And I meant it.

He smiled.

Not big.

Not showy.

Just real.

And then he kissed me.

Soft.

Like he always did.

Like he wasn't taking anything—just meeting me there.

Later, we stood near the door again.

The night quieter now.

"Do you want to Uber home and come get my car tomorrow?" he asked.

A pause.

"Or we can stay. They've got rooms blocked off."

He didn't step closer.

Didn't reach for me.

Just stood there.

Waiting.

Letting it be my choice.

And that felt different.

Not like before.

Not like something I had to decide quickly.

Not like something I had to say yes to.

It was possibility.

"I want to stay," I said quietly.

He nodded. "Okay."

No shift.

No expectation.

Just okay.

The room was quiet when we got inside.

Dimly lit.

Calm.

Everything slowed the second the door closed behind us.

For a moment, we just stood there.

Looking at each other.

Like neither of us wanted to rush past it.

He stepped closer.

Slow.

Giving me time to move away.

I didn't.

Because for the first time, I didn't feel like I needed to.

His hand found mine again.

Familiar now.

Safe.

And when he kissed me, it unraveled gently.

Not rushed.

Not overwhelming.

Not something I felt like I had to give into.

It felt like something I was choosing too.

Everything about it was slower.

More careful.

Like he was paying attention.

Like he didn't want to cross a line—unless I moved it.

And I did.

Not because I felt like I had to.

Not because I was trying to prove anything.

But because I wanted to.

Because for the first time, I felt like I was part of it.

Not losing myself in it.

The room stayed quiet.

The moment stayed soft.

And somewhere in the middle of it, something in me shifted.

Not fully.

Not completely.

But enough to feel it.

Because this didn't feel like before.

It didn't feel like pressure.

Or control.

Or something I had to keep up with.

It felt real.

Later, I lay there—the room still.

His arm around me.

My chest full.

Not heavy.

Just full.

And that scared me.

Because I knew what this feeling meant.

Even if I didn't want to say it yet.

I was falling for him.

And I didn't know if I was ready for that.

TWENTY-TWO
WHEN IT'S QUIET

Morning came softly.

Light filtered through the curtains in thin, warm lines.

For a second, I didn't move.

Just lay there.

Letting the stillness settle around me.

And then I noticed it.

The quiet.

Too quiet.

My eyes opened slowly.

The room looked different in daylight.

Calm.

But empty.

I turned slightly.

The bed beside me—cold.

My throat closed instantly.

Not slowly.

Not rationally.

Just there.

I sat up too fast.

The room spinning slightly as everything rushed back.

Last night.

The way it felt.

The way it didn't feel like before.

The way I let myself believe—just for a second—that something could be different.

And now he was gone.

My stomach dropped.

Of course.

The thought came fast.

Too familiar.

That makes sense.

I swallowed hard.

Because this was how it always went.

Good.

Until it wasn't.

I pulled the blanket tighter around me, my heart beating harder than it should have.

You knew better.

The voice in my head was quiet—but sharp.

You always do this.

You let yourself believe it was different.

I shook my head slightly.

No.

No, this wasn't—

But the feeling didn't stop.

Because the quiet felt the same.

The empty space felt the same.

And my body didn't know the difference yet.

I swung my legs over the side of the bed, standing too quickly.

Grabbing my phone.

Nothing.

No message.

No note.

My chest dropped again.

Because of course—why would there be?

I ran a hand through my hair, pacing slightly.

Trying to slow it down.

Trying to make it make sense.

He left.

The thought landed heavier this time.

He left and didn't say anything.

You should've known.

I stopped.

Mid-step.

Because something in me—barely—pushed back.

No.

It was quieter.

Weaker.

But it was there.

That's not what this felt like.

I exhaled sharply.

Trying to hold onto that.

Trying to separate what was real from what I was used to.

And then the door opened.

I froze.

Wes stepped inside.

Coffee in one hand.

A small paper bag in the other.

"Hey," he said, like nothing was wrong. "I didn't want to wake you."

I blinked.

My chest still tight.

But shifting.

"You left," I said.

It came out before I could stop it.

Quieter than I meant it to be.

But still there.

He paused.

Just for a second.

Then: "I went to grab coffee," he said gently, holding it up slightly.

Like that explained everything.

Because to him, it did.

"I didn't want to wake you up," he added.

And just like that, everything in me stilled.

The panic.

The spiral.

All of it felt too loud now.

Too quick.

"Oh," I said.

My shoulders dropping slightly.

"I just—"

I stopped.

Because I didn't even know how to explain it.

Not in a way that made sense.

He set the coffee down on the table, stepping a little closer.

Not too close.

Just enough.

"You okay?" he asked.

And the way he said it—not assuming anything, not accusing, just asking—made my chest loosen.

"Yeah," I said.

A small pause.

"Just not used to that."

His expression softened slightly.

But he didn't overreact.

Didn't question it.

Didn't make it bigger than it was.

"Okay," he said.

Just that.

And somehow, that helped more than anything else.

He handed me the coffee.

My fingers brushing his briefly.

Warm.

Steady.

Still there.

I sat back down on the edge of the bed, wrapping my hands around the cup.

Letting the warmth sink in.

Letting myself breathe again.

Because even though nothing had actually gone wrong, it had felt like it did.

And that scared me more than anything else.

Because if something this small—this normal—could feel like that, then I didn't know how I was supposed to trust any of it.

I glanced up at him.

Still there.

Still the same.

And for a second, I let myself believe it.

Just a little.

TWENTY-THREE
DON'T PULL AWAY

The shift was small.

Barely noticeable.

But it was there.

In the way I answered him.

Shorter.

Quieter.

More careful than before.

Like I was trying not to get too close again.

We were supposed to leave Friday morning.

Up north.

My parents' cabin.

And I should've been excited.

I had been.

Until that morning.

Until the quiet.

Until the feeling that something had already gone wrong—even though it hadn't.

"You're still good for this weekend, right?" I asked.

We were on the couch.

Bella curled up between us.

"Yeah," he said.

Simple.

But my throat caught anyway.

"You don't have to go if you don't want to," I added quickly.

Too quickly.

His brows pulled together slightly. "Why wouldn't I want to?"

I shrugged. "I don't know. It's just... a lot."

He studied me for a second.

"Anna," he said, quieter now. "What's going on?"

"Nothing."

Too fast.

He shook his head slightly. "It's not nothing."

I exhaled sharply.

Because I didn't know how to explain this without it sounding like too much.

"I need you to do something," I said.

He didn't hesitate. "Okay."

That almost made it worse.

I swallowed. "I need you to block him."

A pause.

"Stephen," I added quickly. "And... anyone connected to him."

His expression didn't change—but I could see him trying to understand.

"His friends. His family. Anything," I said. "If there's even a chance they could find you"

My voice caught slightly.

"I just need it gone."

The room went quiet.

And suddenly I felt it.

How it sounded.

Too much.

Too intense.

Too—

"I know that sounds—" I started.

"No," he said gently.

And just like that, I stopped.

"I get why you'd feel that way," he said.

His voice stayed calm.

Grounded.

Not dismissing it.

Not feeding it either.

"I just don't want anything touching this," I said.

My chest tightening again.

"I don't want him finding you. Or knowing about you. Or—"

I shook my head.

"Ruining this before it even gets a chance."

Because that was the truth.

Not just that he might leave—but that something else, something I couldn't control, would take it from me.

Wes didn't respond right away.

He reached for his phone.

Opened it.

Scrolled.

Blocked.

One by one.

No questions.

No hesitation.

"I'll take care of it," he said.

Simple.

My chest loosened slightly.

"Okay," I said.

He set his phone down.

Then looked at me.

"You don't have to carry that by yourself," he said.

Not fixing it.

Just meeting me in it.

And for a second, I believed him.

But the fear didn't disappear.

It just quieted.

Enough to move forward.

TWENTY-FOUR
UP NORTH

The drive felt different.

Longer.

Quieter.

But not in a bad way.

Matt drove.

Mallory sat in the front, her feet tucked up slightly, talking to him like they had been doing it forever.

They had fallen into something easy.

And watching it—watching my brother like that—felt good.

Wes sat next to me.

His hand resting loosely over mine.

Not holding on.

Just there.

The cabin came into view slowly.

Tucked between trees.

Familiar in a way that hit me instantly.

Home.

"You made it," my mom said, pulling me into a hug the second I stepped out.

Then her eyes moved.

To him.

"You must be Wes," she said.

He smiled. "Yeah."

She stepped forward, hugging him like she already knew him.

And somehow, that didn't feel strange.

"It's so nice to finally meet you," she said.

Finally.

The word stuck with me.

Because that's what this was.

Something real enough to bring home.

My dad came out a second later.

More reserved.

But still watching.

Sizing him up in that quiet way he always did.

"Wes," he said, holding out his hand.

Wes shook it.

Firm.

Respectful.

"Yes, sir."

My dad nodded slightly.

And just like that, I saw it.

Approval.

Not loud.

But there.

Matt clapped Wes on the shoulder as they passed each other.

"Try not to embarrass me this weekend," Matt said casually.

Wes smirked slightly. "No promises."

Mallory laughed.

And just like that, it felt effortless.

Dinner came together the way it always did.

Too many people in the kitchen.

Too many conversations at once.

And somehow, Wes fit right into it.

He helped without being asked.

Grabbed plates.

Poured drinks.

Listened.

Actually listened.

My mom noticed.

Of course she did.

I could see it in the way she watched him when he wasn't looking.

My dad asked him questions.

Where he went to school.

What he wanted to do.

And Wes didn't rush through the answers.

Didn't boast.

Just answered.

Steady.

Dinner spread out across the table.

Steaming bowls.

Laughter louder now.

Stories overlapping.

And for the first time in a long time, I didn't feel like I had to read the room.

I didn't feel like I was waiting for something to shift.

I just felt...

Here.

Wes's hand brushed mine under the table.

Quick.

Warm.

Gone just as fast.

But enough.

My mom caught it.

Her eyes softening in a way I recognized.

And later, when things quieted—

She pulled me aside.

"He's good for you," she said quietly.

I nodded.

I knew.

Even if part of me was still learning how to believe it.

TWENTY-FIVE

TOO GOOD

Being up at the cabin felt different at night.

Quieter.

The kind of quiet that didn't make you feel alone—just still.

Peaceful.

Everyone had gone inside.

The lights dimmed.

The sounds softened.

And for once, there was nothing pulling at me.

No noise.

No expectations.

Just him.

Wes sat beside me on the dock, his feet stretched out toward the water.

Mine tucked underneath me.

Close.

But not touching—until his hand found mine.

Like it always did.

Effortless.

We didn't talk right away.

Didn't need to.

The lake was calm.

The sky clear.

And for a second, everything felt perfect.

Not in a big, overwhelming way.

Just right.

"This is my favorite place," I said quietly.

He nodded slightly. "I can see why."

A pause.

"I haven't brought many people here," I added.

The words came out softer than I meant them to.

He glanced over at me. "I'm glad you brought me."

My throat tightened.

Because that meant more than I knew how to explain.

I leaned slightly into him.

Not thinking.

Just doing it.

And he didn't react.

Didn't make it a moment.

Just adjusted slightly so I fit there easier.

Like it was natural.

Like it wasn't something fragile.

And that's when it hit me.

Harder than anything else had.

This could be real.

My pulse raced.

Because that thought was too big.

Too fast.

Too good.

The next morning, things shifted.

Not dramatically.

Just enough.

We were inside, coffee in hand, my parents talking about traffic on the way out.

"Monday's going to be a mess," my dad said. "Everyone leaves at the same time."

Matt nodded. "Yeah, we should probably head out early."

I barely registered it.

Until Wes spoke.

"We could leave before that," he said. "Beat it."

My stomach knotted instantly.

There it was.

I looked at him. "You want to leave early?"

He glanced at me. "Just thinking it might be easier."

Easier.

The word hit wrong.

"Oh," I said.

Too casual.

Too controlled.

He didn't catch it right away.

Of course he didn't.

Because this wasn't about traffic.

It was about the shift.

The same one I had been waiting for.

I stood up, setting my coffee down a little too quickly.

"I mean, you don't have to stay the whole time," I said.

There it was again.

That pullback.

That instinct to give him an out before he could take one.

He looked at me now.

Really looked.

"Anna," he said.

I shrugged slightly. "It's fine if you have other plans."

A pause.

"That's not what this is," he said.

But my chest was already tight.

Already pulling back.

Because I had felt it.

That shift.

Even if it wasn't real.

"It's just traffic," he added.

But that wasn't what it felt like.

"You don't have to explain it," I said quietly.

And that made it worse.

Because now he could feel it.

The distance.

The way I was already stepping back.

"I'm not trying to leave," he said.

My eyes dropped. "Okay."

But it didn't sound like I believed him.

A pause.

Then he stood up.

Stepping a little closer.

Not forcing it.

Just enough.

"I said it because I thought it would make things easier," he said.

His voice calmer now.

More intentional.

"Not because I want to go anywhere."

My chest loosened slightly.

Because part of me knew that.

But the other part—the louder part—didn't.

"I like being here," he added.

A small pause.

"With you."

That one settled something.

Not everything.

But enough.

I exhaled slowly. "I just thought—"

I stopped.

Shook my head.

"Forget it."

"No," he said gently. "Don't do that."

I hesitated.

Then: "It felt like you were trying to leave," I admitted.

My voice quieter now.

More honest.

His expression softened slightly. "I'm not."

And this time, I believed him.

At least a little.

Later, the plans shifted.

They stayed.

Sunday came and went.

Then Monday.

And somehow, it felt easier.

Quieter.

By the last day, it was just us.

Me.

Wes.

Matt.

Mallory.

The cabin slower.

Less noise.

Less movement.

And something in me finally started to settle.

Because he didn't leave.

Didn't pull away.

Didn't shift.

He stayed.

Through all of it.

And even though the fear didn't disappear—it softened.

Just enough.

TWENTY-SIX
STAY

Time had passed.

Not rushed.

Not forced.

Just naturally.

Weeks turned into months.

And somehow, he was still there.

It had been almost a year.

Nothing had fallen apart.

Not the way I expected.

Not the way I kept waiting for it to.

Mallory was barely at the apartment anymore.

Between Matt and everything else, it just made sense.

For him to be there more.

"You could just move in," I said one night.

The words slipped out casually.

Too casually.

He looked at me. "Yeah?" he asked.

I shrugged. "Mallory's never here. You basically are anyway."

A pause.

"It would just make sense."

He didn't answer right away.

And that small pause hit something in me.

Too long.

Too familiar.

"You don't have to," I added quickly.

There it was again.

That instinct.

Pulling it back before it could be taken from me.

"I wasn't saying no," he said.

But I was already shifting.

Already reading into it.

Already deciding what it meant.

"It's fine," I said.

Too flat.

Too controlled.

He sat up slightly. "Anna."

I didn't look at him.

Because I could feel it.

That moment.

The one where everything starts to change.

"I just don't want to make this into something it's not," I said.

There it was.

The line I always used.

The one that made it easier to step back.

"What is that supposed to mean?" he asked.

His voice still calm.

But different.

I shrugged again. "It just feels like a lot."

"A lot because you don't want it," he said.

A pause.

"Or because you think I don't?"

"That's not what I said."

"But that's what you're doing," he said.

And this time, I looked at him.

Because something had shifted.

Not in the way I feared.

In a way I didn't expect.

"I'm trying," he said.

Not loudly.

Not aggressively.

Just honestly.

"I've been trying," he added.

My throat tightened.

"And it feels like you're already deciding how this ends before I even get the chance to be in it."

The words hit harder than anything else.

Because they were true.

"I'm not—" I started.

"Yes, you are," he said.

Still calm.

Still controlled.

But something real underneath now.

"You pull away every time something gets good," he said.

"Every time it starts to feel real—"

He stopped.

Ran a hand through his hair.

"You act like it's already over."

The room felt too quiet.

Too still.

"I don't know how not to," I said.

And that was the truth.

Because I didn't.

A pause.

Then: "I'm not him, Anna," he said.

Soft.

Not defensive.

Just clear.

"I know," I said.

But my voice didn't sound convinced.

"And I feel like I'm constantly trying to prove that to you," he added.

"But you don't let me."

That one broke something open.

Because I could feel it.

The way I did that.

The way I held back.

The way I protected myself—even when I didn't need to anymore.

"I'm scared," I said.

The words quieter than anything else.

"I know," he said.

"But you don't get to push me away because of that."

A pause.

"I'm still here."

And for the first time, that didn't feel like something I had to question.

It felt like something I could hold onto.

"I want this," he said.

Simple.

Clear.

"I want you."

My chest swelled.

Because that was the thing I'd been waiting to hear.

Without even realizing it.

"And I'm not going anywhere," he added.

The silence that followed wasn't heavy.

Wasn't tense.

It was real.

I stepped closer.

Not thinking.

Just feeling it.

"I'm trying too," I said.

My voice softer now.

"I know," he said.

And then: "I love you."

The words hit all at once.

Not expected.

Not planned.

Just there.

My heart stuttered.

Because I felt it too.

I just hadn't let myself say it yet.

"I love you," I said.

And this time, no hesitation.

He pulled me into him.

Not rushed.

Not overwhelming.

Just steady.

And when he kissed me, it felt deeper.

Not something I was afraid of.

Something I was part of.

Everything slowed.

Everything softened.

And for the first time, I didn't feel like I had to hold anything back.

I chose it.

And so did he.

TWENTY-SEVEN
MOVING IN

Moving in didn't happen all at once.

It wasn't some big, planned moment.

No boxes stacked in the living room.

No "this is official" conversation.

It just happened.

His sweatshirt stayed.

Then a pair of shoes by the door.

A toothbrush next to mine.

And one night—he didn't leave.

Mallory barely noticed.

Between Matt and everything else, it just made sense.

"You live here now," she said one night, grabbing her bag.

Wes laughed. "Guess so."

She looked at me. "You good with that?"

I hesitated.

Just for a second.

Then: "Yeah."

And I meant it.

Mostly.

The first few days felt effortless.

Routine settled in without asking.

Coffee in the morning.

Him moving around the kitchen like he'd always been there.

Bella following him like he belonged to her now.

It should've felt overwhelming.

Too much.

Too fast.

But it didn't.

It felt right.

And that still caught me off guard.

"You're staring again," he said one morning.

I blinked. "What?"

"You do that," he smiled, "like you're trying to figure something out."

"Where's your head at, pretty girl?"

I shook my head slightly.

"Just thinking."

About how this didn't feel like before.

About how I wasn't waiting for something to go wrong every second.

But I didn't say that out loud.

Still, the moments came.

Small.

Unexpected.

Like when he didn't text back right away.

Or when he got quiet for too long.

Or when he left the room without saying anything.

My stomach would flutter.

Not as sharp as before.

But still familiar.

And every time, I felt it.

That instinct.

To pull back.

To protect myself before something could hurt me.

But now, there was something else too.

Something quieter.

Stay.

One night, he was running late.

Nothing big.

He texted.

Told me he'd be home soon.

But *soon* felt longer than it should have.

I sat on the couch.

Bella curled next to me.

The apartment too quiet.

And I could feel it again.

That shift.

That old, familiar feeling creeping in.

Something's off.

My fingers tightened around my phone.

You know how this goes.

I stood up.

Started pacing.

Because it always started like this.

Small.

Until it wasn't.

The door opened.

And I froze.

Wes walked in like nothing was wrong.

"Hey," he said.

And just like that, everything in me settled.

"You're late," I said.

It came out sharper than I meant it to.

He paused. "Yeah, I told you I'd be a little late."

"I know," I said quickly.

Too quickly.

A pause.

Then: "You okay?" he asked.

I hesitated.

And for the first time, I didn't say *I'm fine*.

"I thought something was wrong," I admitted.

My voice quieter now.

His expression softened. "Nothing's wrong," he said.

Simple.

I nodded.

And this time, I believed him.

Because he didn't get defensive.

Didn't turn it around on me.

Didn't make me feel crazy for feeling it.

He just stayed.

"I'm still getting used to this," I said.

He stepped closer. "I know."

And that was it.

No lecture.

No frustration.

Just understanding.

Later that night, we sat on the couch.

Closer than before.

More natural.

His arm around me.

My head resting against his shoulder.

And for once, I didn't feel like I had to question it.

Not because the fear was gone—but because I was learning, slowly, how to stay anyway.

TWENTY-EIGHT
BIG MACS

The night started easy.

Too easy.

We had tickets to a concert.

A band we both loved.

And for whatever reason, it felt like something that belonged to both of us.

Not just his world.

Not just mine.

Ours.

"Ready?" he asked, keys in hand.

I nodded. "Yeah."

But my stomach was already fluttering.

Because I knew who would be there.

His friends.

The venue was loud.

Crowded.

Music pulsing through the walls before we even stepped inside.

Vinny waved us over first.

Kyler next to him.

Avery close by.

And then Duke.

"Look who made it," he said, already a little buzzed.

I smiled. "Hi."

Wes's hand found my lower back.

Light.

Steady.

Grounding.

And for a second, I felt okay.

The music started.

The crowd surged.

Everyone moving.

Dancing.

Singing.

And slowly, I let myself fall into it.

A drink.

Then another.

The tension softened.

Just enough.

I laughed more.

Talked more.

Didn't overthink every word.

At one point, Duke leaned in, yelling something over the music.

I laughed.

Shook my head.

Answered back.

Nothing.

Harmless.

But when I turned, Wes was watching.

Not angry.

Not upset.

Just looking.

And instantly, my throat tightened.

There it was.

That feeling.

The shift.

You're doing too much.

He thinks you're flirting.

I pulled back slightly.

Moved closer to Wes.

Too aware now.

Too careful.

"Hey," he said, leaning closer. "You good?"

"Yeah," I said quickly.

Too quickly.

But the rest of the night, I felt it.

That pressure.

That awareness.

Like I'd already done something wrong—even if I hadn't.

The drive home was quieter.

Not tense.

Just different.

Wes drove.

One hand on the wheel.

The other resting loosely near mine.

I stared out the window.

Lights blurring past.

Trying to shake the feeling.

But it stayed.

"You got quiet," he said.

I exhaled. "I feel like I did something wrong."

He glanced over. "What?"

"With Duke," I said.

The words felt stupid leaving my mouth.

He frowned slightly. "What are you talking about?"

"I don't know," I said.

My voice softer now.

"I just felt like you were watching me."

A pause.

"I *was* watching you," he said.

My stomach dropped.

"But not like that," he added quickly.

I looked at him.

"I was watching you have fun," he said.

Simple.

"I wasn't upset."

The silence hit different.

Because that's not what I expected.

"I thought you thought I was—" I stopped.

"Flirting?" he finished.

I nodded slightly.

He shook his head. "No."

Just that.

My chest loosened.

"I wouldn't just assume that about you," he added.

And that landed deeper than anything.

Because I was used to that.

Being questioned.

Being watched.

Turned into something I wasn't doing.

"I didn't realize I still did that," I said quietly.

"Did what?"

"Assume I already messed something up."

He was quiet for a second.

Then: "You're allowed to have fun."

My throat tightened slightly.

And for the first time, I believed it.

The car slowed.

Turned.

And then he pulled into McDonald's.

I blinked. "What are you doing?"

He smiled slightly. "Big Macs."

I laughed. "Right now?"

"Yeah."

I shook my head. "You're ridiculous."

"After concerts," he said, "or weddings—anything like that—this is the move."

I laughed again.

Because it made no sense.

But somehow, it did.

We sat in the car.

Windows slightly cracked.

The smell of fries filling the space.

I took a bite.

Still laughing a little.

"This is so random."

He smiled. "Yeah."

A pause.

"But it's ours now."

My heart stuttered softly.

Because it didn't have to mean anything.

But it did.

Simple.

Easy.

Ours.

And for the first time that night, I didn't feel like I had to question it.

I just enjoyed it.

TWENTY-NINE

MARCH MADNESS

Things felt steady.

Not overwhelming.

Just right.

The apartment was louder than usual.

Voices filled the living room.

Shoes scattered by the door.

Wes had people over.

Not just a couple.

A full house.

March Madness played on the TV.

Everyone yelling at the screen like it mattered more than anything.

And somehow, I wasn't on the outside of it.

"Anna, you want another drink?" Vinny called from the kitchen.

"Yeah," I said, standing up.

"Got you," he nodded.

Avery smiled at me from the couch. "I think your team's losing."

"I don't even have a team. I just picked the prettiest jerseys," I laughed.

"Oh my god, Anna," she said. "You can't just fill out your bracket that way."

I smiled. "Why not? It's not like I'm going to win anyway."

And somehow, that felt normal.

Not forced.

Not watched.

Just included.

Wes walked past, his hand brushing my back.

Small.

Unnoticed by anyone else.

But I felt it.

Always.

"You good?" he asked quietly.

I nodded. "Yeah."

And this time, I didn't hesitate.

Because I was.

I sat back down.

Bella curled at my feet.

Avery leaning into Kyler beside me.

Vinny laughing too loud across the room.

Wes somewhere behind—talking, moving, existing so naturally in all of this.

And for a second, I just took it in.

Because this was his world.

And I wasn't just standing in it anymore.

I was part of it.

No one watching too closely.

No one waiting for me to mess up.

No one trying to control how I acted, who I talked to, what I said.

I could just be.

And I didn't even realize how much that mattered—until I felt it.

"Come here," Wes said, reaching for my hand as he sat next to me.

I shifted easily, tucking into his side without thinking.

Natural.

Effortless.

The game got louder.

Everyone yelling again.

But I wasn't paying attention.

Because warmth spread through my chest.

Not tight.

Not heavy.

Just full.

"You okay?" he asked again, quieter.

I nodded. "Yeah."

A small pause.

"This feels different."

He looked down at me. "How?"

I hesitated.

Because I didn't know how to explain it without sounding like I was realizing something I should've known.

"I don't feel like I'm trying," I said finally.

The words soft.

Honest.

His expression shifted slightly.

Not confused.

Just listening.

"I don't feel like I have to watch everything I say," I added.

My fingers tracing lightly along his arm.

"Or think about how it looks. Or if I'm doing something wrong."

A pause.

"I just feel like I'm here."

And that was everything.

His hand tightened slightly around mine.

Not pulling.

Just holding.

"You are," he said.

Simple.

And for once, I didn't question it.

The game ended.

People started moving.

More noise.

More chaos.

But it didn't feel overwhelming.

Because I wasn't trying to find my place anymore.

I had one.

Later that night, after everyone left, the apartment felt quiet again.

But not empty.

We cleaned up together.

Easy.

Passing each other in the kitchen.

Small touches.

Small moments.

And then we ended up on the couch.

Just us.

My head rested against his chest.

His hand moving slowly along my arm.

"You're different tonight," he said.

I smiled slightly. "Good different?"

"Yeah."

A pause.

"Comfortable."

Warmth spread through me again.

"I think I am," I said.

And that felt bigger than anything else.

Because for so long, comfort had meant something else.

Something controlled.

Something temporary.

But this felt like something I could stay in.

Not something I had to survive.

"I like this," I said quietly.

He didn't respond right away.

Didn't make it a big moment.

He just pressed a soft kiss to the top of my head.

"Me too."

And that was it.

No pressure.

No expectations.

Just two people sitting in something real.

And I wasn't waiting for it to fall apart.

I was just in it.

THIRTY
IN THE RAIN

It started small.

It always did.

At first, I didn't even notice it.

Wes coming home quieter.

Shorter answers.

A little more distant in a way I couldn't quite place.

Not gone.

Just not the same.

"You okay?" I asked one night.

"Yeah," he said.

Too quick.

Too flat.

And something in my chest shifted.

The days that followed felt heavier.

He worked later.

Texted less.

And my mind did what it always did.

Something's wrong. He's pulling away.

You know how this ends.

I tried to ignore it.

Tried to be normal.

But when he came home late again, something in me snapped.

"Where were you?" I asked.

"At work," he said.

"No you weren't."

His brows pulled together. "What are you talking about?"

"You've been off all week," I said.

My voice rising without meaning to.

"You don't answer me, you're short, you're—"

"I'm not—" he started.

But his voice lifted.

Just slightly.

And that was all it took.

My body reacted before I could stop it.

"There it is," I said, backing up.

"There what is?" he asked.

"This," I said. "You're already changing."

His expression shifted.

Not angry.

Frustrated.

"Anna—"

"No," I cut him off.

Because I couldn't slow it down.

"I knew this would happen," I said.

My voice breaking.

"I knew it was too good and now you're just—what? Done? Talking to someone else?"

His face dropped. "What?"

I grabbed my keys.

"I'm not doing this."

"Doing what?" he asked.

"This," I said. "Waiting for you to leave."

And before he could stop me, I was outside.

The rain hit instantly.

Cold.

Heavy.

Soaking through everything.

I walked straight to my car—fumbling with the handle—my hands shaking.

"Anna!"

His voice behind me.

Closer.

"Stop."

I turned.

Finally.

"I'm trying so hard," I said.

The words ripping out of me.

"I am holding on for dear life—"

My voice cracked.

"And I'm just waiting."

The rain blurred everything.

"Waiting for you to walk away," I said.

My chest heaving.

"Waiting for you to decide I'm too much."

Silence.

Just rain.

And then he moved.

Fast.

His hands found my face—cold, soaked, steady—

and he kissed me.

Not soft.

Not hesitant.

Certain.

Grounding.

Like he was stopping everything from unraveling.

"I'm not going anywhere," he said against my lips.

"I choose you," he said.

Clear.

Firm.

"You are my person."

The rain didn't matter anymore.

"You're everything to me," he said.

"I don't know how else to prove that to you."

My hands clutched his shirt.

Holding on.

"I'm in love with you," he said.

And something in me finally gave in.

Not fear.

Not panic.

Just trust.

He lifted me—like it was nothing—

carrying me back inside.

Both of us soaked.

Laughing through tears.

And for the first time, there was no fear in it.

Later, the rain slowed.

Then stopped.

We lay there—quiet.

Breathing settling.

Everything softer.

I let out a small laugh.

"Should we get Big Macs?" he asked.

I smiled. "Obviously."

The drive-through line was long.

Of course it was.

I sat in the passenger seat.

His hand wrapped around mine.

Lifting it.

Kissing my knuckles.

The radio hummed quietly.

And then *She Will Be Loved* played.

I smiled.

Turning it up.

He glanced over.

Soft smile.

"I could do this with you forever," he said.

Simple.

My heart swelled.

Because this time, it didn't scare me the same way.

"Just this," he added. "Stuff like this."

A small pause.

"I can see myself doing this with you for the rest of my life."

We pulled into a parking spot.

Unwrapping food.

Laughing.

Talking like we always did.

And right there—in that moment—

it didn't feel like something I was going to lose.

It felt like something I could have.

THIRTY-ONE
WHERE I FIT

It didn't happen all at once.

There wasn't a moment where everything suddenly clicked.

It just shifted.

Slowly.

Quietly.

Until one day, I looked around and realized everything had come together.

The apartment felt different now.

Not just mine.

Not just his.

Ours.

But it wasn't just that.

It was everything around it.

The people.

His friends weren't just his anymore.

Vinny texting me about plans.

Avery sending things she knew I'd like.

Kyler making jokes like I'd always been part of it.

And somewhere along the way, it stopped feeling like I was stepping into something.

It started feeling like I belonged there.

Not because anyone said it.

But because no one questioned it.

It just was.

And my friends—old and new—weren't separate anymore either.

Mallory and Matt were their own thing now.

Blended into everything.

But even beyond that, Wes fit into my world in a way that felt just as natural.

Like there was never a divide to begin with.

Like we weren't two separate lives trying to make something work—we were just building one.

There were nights at the apartment that felt loud in the best way.

Music playing.

People moving in and out of rooms.

Voices layered over each other.

I wasn't overthinking where to stand.

Or what to say.

Or who I should be in it.

I just was.

And no one looked at me like I didn't belong.

No one made me feel like I had to earn my place.

No one made me question if I was too much or not enough.

I caught myself laughing one night—really laughing—at something stupid Vinny said.

And it hit me.

Not all at once.

But enough to feel it.

This is what it's supposed to feel like.

Easy.

Not forced.

Not something I had to constantly keep up with.

Just real.

Wes moved around all of it like he always had.

Comfortable.

Steady.

But now, I wasn't watching him from the outside anymore.

I was next to him.

Part of it.

Part of everything.

His hand finding mine without thinking.

My body leaning into his the same way.

Not second-guessing it.

Not questioning if it meant something more.

Because it already did.

And that didn't scare me the same way.

Later that night, after everyone left, the apartment felt quiet again.

But not empty.

Never empty anymore.

We sat on the couch.

My legs draped over his.

His hand resting along my arm.

"You're different," he said softly.

I smiled. "I know."

A small pause.

"I think I finally feel like I fit."

The words came out quieter than I expected—but they felt right.

He didn't say anything.

Just pulled me a little closer,

like he already understood.

And for the first time, I wasn't holding everything together.

I wasn't waiting for it to fall apart.

I wasn't standing on the outside, hoping I wouldn't lose it.

I was in it.

Fully.

And it felt like something I could finally keep.

THIRTY-TWO
FOREVER STARTS HERE

It didn't start the way I expected.

No big speech.

No warning.

Just: "Pack a bag."

I blinked. "What?"

Wes stood in the doorway, keys in hand, that small smile like he already knew I'd question it.

"Lexie's coming to stay with Bella," he said. "We're leaving in an hour."

I laughed. "Where are we going?"

"Just pack a bag. Let's go!"

I narrowed my eyes. "You're being suspicious."

"I'm being fun," he corrected.

I smiled.

Because he was.

And I didn't question it.

The drive started easy.

Music low.

Windows cracked.

The kind of road trip that didn't feel planned—just right.

"Wait," I said suddenly.

He glanced over. "What?"

"You're Canadian."

He laughed. "Yeah."

"And you've never taken me to Toronto?"

He shook his head. "I guess I haven't."

I looked at him. "Is that where we're going?"

A pause.

A smirk.

"Maybe."

I laughed. "Wes."

But when the skyline came into view, something in me lit up.

"Shut up," I said.

He smiled.

"Oh my God—you're taking me to Toronto."

And just like that, I felt it.

That lightness.

That excitement.

The kind I was starting to recognize.

The weekend felt like something out of a different life.

We went everywhere.

CN Tower—standing at the top, the city stretched beneath us.

"You good?" he asked as I stepped carefully across the glass floor.

"Barely," I laughed.

His hand stayed in mine the whole time.

Hockey Hall of Fame—him explaining things I didn't fully understand, but listening anyway—because he loved it.

Casa Loma—walking through quiet halls frozen in time.

And every moment felt effortless.

I wasn't overthinking.

I wasn't trying to keep up.

I just fit.

That night, we got ready for dinner.

The hotel room quiet.

Soft light.

The city glowing outside the windows.

"I'll be quick," I said, grabbing my dress and heading into the bathroom.

When I stepped back out—everything shifted.

He was there.

In the middle of the room.

On one knee.

For a second, I didn't move.

Didn't breathe.

Because it didn't feel real.

"Wes..." I whispered.

He smiled.

Nervous.

Not perfectly composed.

Just him.

"I had this whole plan," he said softly.

A small laugh under his breath.

"Something bigger.

Something more put together."

He shook his head slightly.

"But this—"

His eyes met mine.

"This feels more like us."

My chest cracked open.

"I don't want perfect," he said.

"I just want you."

Tears blurred my vision instantly.

"I want the random drives.

The concerts.

The Big Macs in parking lots."

A small smile pulled through my tears.

"I want the good days.

The hard days.

The ones we don't understand yet."

My chest felt like it might cave in.

"I want to wake up next to you every day."

His voice softer now.

"Not because it's easy—"

A pause.

"But because it's you."

I couldn't stop the tears now.

"You're my person," he said.

Simple.

Certain.

"I choose you.

Every time."

And this time, I didn't question it.

"I love you, Anna."

The words landed deep.

Steady.

"Will you marry me?"

The room went still.

Like everything had paused—just for this moment.

And for the first time, I wasn't waiting for it to fall apart.

I stepped closer.

Barely able to see through the tears.

"Yes," I said.

My voice breaking.

"Yes."

He stood quickly—laughing a little—pulling me into him.

The ring slid onto my finger.

Perfect.

Like it had always been.

THIRTY-THREE
I GET TO HAVE THIS

I couldn't stop looking at it.

Even when I tried—my eyes found it again.

My hand resting in my lap.

The ring catching the light just enough to remind me it was real.

I sat curled up on the hotel bed, my phone already in my hand.

"Call her," Wes said, smiling from across the room.

"I am," I said.

But I didn't move.

Because I didn't even know how to say it yet.

The phone rang.

Once.

Twice.

Lexie's face popped onto the screen.

"Hi—"

She stopped.

Her eyes dropped.

Straight to my hand.

"Shut up."

I laughed instantly. "I can't."

"SHUT. UP."

I held my hand up to the camera.

And that was it.

She screamed.

Actually screamed.

"Oh my God. Oh my God. OH MY GOD."

I was laughing.

Crying.

Not even trying to hide it.

"Show me again," she said, leaning closer.

"Lex, you're seeing it."

"I need to see it again."

I turned my hand slightly—watching it the same way she was.

Like I still didn't believe it.

"When did this happen?" she asked.

"Just now," I said.

"Like... just now now."

Her expression softened.

And that look—that one—hit me.

Because she knew.

What it took to get here.

"I'm so happy for you," she said.

Quiet now.

Real.

I swallowed, tears slipping down my face. "Me too."

Wes stepped into frame behind me, wrapping his arm around my shoulders.

Lexie pointed at him immediately. "You better not ever hurt her."

He laughed softly. "I won't."

"Good."

And just like that—it felt complete.

Calling my parents felt different.

Quieter.

Heavier in the best way.

My mom answered right away. "Hi—"

She stopped.

Just like Lexie had.

"Oh my God," she whispered.

I held my hand up.

That was all it took.

Her hand flew to her mouth.

Tears filling her eyes instantly.

"Is this real?" she asked.

I nodded. "Yeah."

My dad stepped into frame behind her. "What's going on?"

She turned the phone.

Showed him.

And for a second, he didn't say anything.

Just looked.

Really looked.

Not surprised.

Not confused.

Like he had been waiting for this.

Then he let out a small breath.

His eyes softening in a way I didn't see often.

"I was wondering how long he was going to wait," he said quietly.

My chest tightened.

Because that meant something.

"He asked me months ago," my dad added.

Simple.

Like it wasn't a big deal.

But it was.

My breath caught. "You knew?"

He nodded. "Of course I did."

A small pause.

"I wouldn't have said yes if I didn't think he was the right man for you."

That was it.

No big speech.

No dramatic moment.

Just certainty.

"He's a good man, Anna."

My chest tightened again—but this time, it felt different.

Not fear.

Not waiting.

Just peace.

"Congratulations," he added.

And I could hear it.

The pride.

The approval.

Wes stood beside me again.

My dad nodded at him.

And just like that—everything aligned.

Mallory didn't even answer.

She FaceTimed back immediately.

"You didn't even text me first?" she said dramatically.

"I needed to process it," I laughed.

"Show me."

I did.

She screamed.

Matt's voice came from somewhere behind her. "What's going on?"

She turned the phone. "Look."

He froze.

Then: "No way."

I laughed. "Yes way."

He shook his head, smiling. "I knew it."

Mallory was already talking a mile a minute.

"What are we doing? When's the wedding? What's the plan—"

"Relax," I laughed.

But I could feel it.

That excitement.

That energy building.

Everything coming together.

The drive home felt quieter.

Not empty.

Just peaceful.

I sat in the passenger seat.

My hand in his.

Still looking at it.

"You're doing it again," he said, smiling.

"I know," I laughed. "I can't stop."

He lifted my hand—pressed a soft kiss to my knuckles.

And that did something to me every time.

"You're really stuck with me now," he teased.

I smiled. "Good."

The road stretched ahead of us.

Familiar.

But everything felt different.

Because I wasn't wondering anymore.

Wasn't waiting for something to go wrong.

I was just here.

With him.

And for the first time, I could breathe.

I wasn't fighting to keep it.

I looked down at my hand again.

Then back at him.

And softly—almost to myself—

"I get to have this."

He glanced over. "What?"

I smiled. "Nothing."

But inside, it meant everything.

THIRTY-FOUR
FALLING INTO PLACE

It all started happening at once.

Not slowly.

Not carefully.

Just all at once.

The job came first.

A real one.

Not juggling two things.

Not barely making it work.

A career.

Something stable.

Something I could be proud of.

"I got it," I said, standing in the middle of the apartment.

Wes looked up immediately. "You did?"

I nodded. "I got it."

And just like that, he pulled me into him.

Laughing.

Spinning me slightly like it was the biggest thing in the world.

Because to me, it was.

Everything started to feel possible.

The wedding planning came next.

Not overwhelming.

Exciting.

Guest lists scribbled on paper.

Venues bookmarked.

Late nights on the couch with my laptop open—

Wes beside me, half paying attention but still there for every decision.

"What about this one?" I asked.

He leaned over. "Too fancy."

I laughed. "Too fancy?"

"Yeah," he said. "That's not us."

And he was right.

Cake tastings.

Too sweet.

Too plain.

Too something.

Until one just felt right.

"This one," I said.

He nodded. "Yeah. That one."

Simple decisions.

But they felt big.

Because they were ours.

Figuring out who would stand beside us—

Lexie.

Of course.

There was never a question.

Mallory—

now more than just my roommate.

More than just my friend.

Family.

Matt would stand beside Wes and all his friends.

And somehow, that felt just as right.

Because everything was starting to connect.

A couple weeks later, Matt proved it.

We were all at the apartment.

Nothing special.

Just another night.

Until Mallory walked in.

Hand over her mouth.

Tears already falling.

"What happened?" I asked, standing too fast.

She held out her hand.

And there it was.

A ring.

I gasped. "No way."

Matt stepped in behind her—grinning like he couldn't hold it in.

"I couldn't wait," he said.

Everyone laughed.

But my heart swelled.

Because that felt bigger than just another moment.

It felt like everything aligning.

"You just didn't want to be the last one," Wes said, shaking his head.

Matt laughed. "Can you blame me?"

Mallory pulled me into a hug.

"We're doing this together," she said.

And just like that, it became something more.

Not just me.

All of us.

The excitement built quickly after that.

Group chats blowing up.

Venues booked.

Dates set.

Double planning.

Double everything.

And somehow, it didn't feel overwhelming.

It felt like life.

The good kind.

Late nights turned into conversations about the future.

Where we'd live.

What things would look like.

Not in a pressured way.

Just naturally.

I caught myself doing it sometimes.

Looking at him—and seeing it.

A life.

Not imagined.

Real.

And I didn't pull away from it.

I leaned in.

"You're staring again," he said one night.

I smiled. "I know."

"What is it this time?" he asked.

I hesitated.

Then: "I just didn't think I'd ever get here."

The words came out softer than I expected.

More honest.

He didn't respond right away.

He just pulled me closer.

And I didn't question it.

Not his intentions.

Not his feelings.

Not what this was.

It all felt clear.

And even though—somewhere deep down—there was still a small part of me that wondered if something could take it all away—

it didn't control me anymore.

Because right now, everything was exactly how it was supposed to be.

And for the first time in my life, I wasn't waiting for it to fall apart.

I was just happy.

THIRTY-FIVE
AND SHE WILL BE LOVED

It wasn't a big moment.

No music playing.

No celebration.

No one watching.

Just a quiet night.

The apartment felt softer than usual.

Warm.

Lived in.

Bella curled up at the end of the couch.

Mallory gone for the night—probably with Matt.

And Wes in the kitchen.

Moving around like he belonged there.

Because he did.

I sat curled up on the couch, my legs tucked underneath me, my hand resting in my lap.

And there it was again.

The ring.

I still looked at it like it might disappear.

Like this life was something I'd borrowed, not something I actually got to keep.

His footsteps moved toward me.

Slow.

Familiar.

He sat beside me, his arm wrapping around me like it always did.

Effortless.

And for once, I didn't think about it.

Didn't analyze it.

Didn't question what it meant.

I just leaned into him.

"I like this," I said quietly.

He glanced down at me. "Yeah?"

I nodded. "Yeah."

A small pause.

"Me too."

The silence that followed wasn't empty.

It was full.

Of everything we had built.

Of everything we had made it through.

And for a second, I let myself go back.

To the girl I used to be.

The one who spent so much time picking up the pieces of her life—that she didn't even realize how broken it had all become.

The one who tried to hold everything together with tape and glue—patching cracks that were never meant to be ignored.

Holding onto things that hurt, because she didn't know how to let them go.

I remembered what that felt like.

Fragile.

Unsteady.

Like one wrong move and everything would fall apart again.

For so long, that was all I knew.

Not whole.

Just held together.

I barely recognized her now.

Not because she was gone—but because she had finally, slowly, painfully, put herself back together the right way.

Not rushed.

Not forced.

Piece by piece.

And somewhere along the way—without even realizing it—I stopped feeling like something that needed to be fixed.

I started to feel whole.

Warmth spread through my chest.

Not from fear.

Not from waiting.

Just feeling it.

"I used to think love was supposed to feel hard," I said quietly.

He didn't interrupt.

Didn't try to fill the space.

"I thought if it wasn't something I had to fight for—"

I shook my head slightly.

"it wasn't real."

A pause.

"But this..."

I looked up at him.

"This feels different."

His hand moved slowly along my arm.

Steady.

Grounding.

"Good different?" he asked.

I smiled. "Yeah."

And then—after a second—"Home."

The word settled between us.

And this time, it didn't scare me.

Because that's what he felt like.

Not chaos.

Not confusion.

Not something I had to survive.

Just home.

He leaned down, pressing a soft kiss to my forehead.

I didn't feel like something was missing.

I didn't feel like I was still searching for the rest of me.

I had it.

This was it.

I rested my head against his chest, listening to the steady rhythm of his breathing.

My mind didn't wander.

Didn't spiral.

Didn't search for what could go wrong.

It just stayed.

"I get to have this," I whispered.

He didn't ask what I meant.

He just held me a little closer.

And that was enough.

Outside, the world kept moving.

Things would change.

They always did.

But in that moment, none of it mattered.

Because right now, I wasn't something broken.

I wasn't something held together.

I was whole.

And for the first time, I finally believed it.

THE REHEARSAL DINNER

The room was full.

Laughter echoed off the walls.

Glasses clinked.

Voices overlapped in a way that felt warm—

not overwhelming.

I stood at the front of the room.

White dress. Soft. Simple.

My hands trembled slightly around the glass I was holding.

And for a second— I couldn't speak.

Because I could see all of them.

Every face.

Every person who had stayed.

Every person who had watched me fall apart—

and somehow helped me find my way back.

My mom sat near the front. Already crying.

My dad beside her— quiet.

Proud.

Lexie.

Of course.

Her eyes locked on mine— steady.

Like they always had been.

Mallory sat next to Matt—

her hand wrapped around his like it had always belonged there.

And Wes— standing beside me.

Dressed in a suit that fit him perfectly. Calm.

Grounded.

Mine.

My chest tightened.

Because for a second— it didn't feel real.

All of this. Everything.

I let out a slow breath.

Trying to steady myself. Trying to find the words.

"I don't really know how to do this," I said softly.

A few quiet laughs moved through the room.

"But that feels kind of fitting."

Because nothing about getting here— had been easy.

My grip tightened slightly around the glass.

"I think... for a long time, I thought I wasn't going to get a moment like this."

My voice wavered— but I didn't stop.

"I thought maybe some people just... don't." The room went quieter.

"And I lost myself along the way," I said.

"I stayed in places I shouldn't have. I believed things about myself that weren't true."

A pause.

"But somehow—"

My voice softened.

"I found my way back."

My eyes shifted.

To him.

Wes was already looking at me.

Not surprised. Not overwhelmed.

Just... there.

"And I didn't do it alone," I said.

"I had people who never gave up on me. Even when I didn't recognize myself anymore."

I glanced at Lexie.

At my parents.

At everyone who had stayed.

"And I don't think I'll ever have the right words to thank you for that."

My voice broke slightly— but I smiled anyway.

"And then I found you."

The room softened. Shifted.

I looked back at Wes. Really looked at him.

"And you showed me what love is supposed to feel like."

"Not something I have to survive."

A tear slipped down my cheek. I didn't wipe it away.

"Something I get to live in." His expression softened.

"And I know it hasn't been easy to get here," I added. "Not for either of us."

"But standing here—"

My voice steadier now—

"I wouldn't change any of it." Because it led me here.

To this.

To him.

"To everyone in this room—" I lifted my glass slightly.

"Thank you for loving me through every version of myself."

A pause.

"And for being here to see the version I fought so hard to become." My chest tightened.

"And to you—"

I turned slightly toward Wes.

"I can't wait to spend the rest of my life choosing you."

The room blurred slightly through my tears.

"Because this—"

I let out a breath.

"This feels like my happily ever after."

The room filled with soft applause. Laughter.

Tears.

But all I could see— was him.

And for a moment— everything felt still.

Perfect.

COMING NEXT IN THE PIECES SERIES

Happily Ever After?

Anna thought she had made it to the other side.

To the part of the story where everything finally settles—

where love is steady,

safe,

and certain.

For the first time,

she isn't waiting for it to fall apart.

She's living in it.

But life doesn't always follow the story we think we're writing.

When an unimaginable loss shakes everything she thought was unbreakable, Anna is forced to face a truth she never wanted to learn—

That love doesn't always protect you from pain.

And sometimes,

the strongest hearts

are the ones that have to break all over again.

Because healing once

doesn't mean you won't have to do it again.

LOOK FOR BOOK 3 IN THE PIECES SERIES

Happily Ever After? SEPTEMBER 2026

She fought to rebuild her life. She found love in the pieces.
She finally believed she was whole.
But happily ever after was never promised.

TAPE & GLUE

Healing doesn't look the way people think it does.

It's not clean.

It's not linear.

And it definitely doesn't happen all at once.

There's this idea that once you leave something that broke you...

that's it.

That you're free.

That you can just move on.

But the truth is—

you carry pieces of it with you.

In the way you think.

In the way you react.

In the way you love.

Tape and Glue was never meant to be a perfect love story.

It was meant to be an honest one.

Because finding something good after something painful doesn't mean everything suddenly feels easy.

Sometimes it means learning how to trust what feels safe... when chaos is what you're used to.

Sometimes it means questioning the very thing you've been hoping for.

Wes is steady.

Patient.

The kind of love people say you deserve.

But when you've only known something different...

even the right kind of love can feel unfamiliar.

And unfamiliar can feel scary.

This book was about that space in between—

between who you were...

and who you're trying to become.

The part no one really talks about.

The part where you're healing,

but still hurting.

Where you're moving forward,

but still looking back.

Where you're learning that love isn't supposed to break you...

but still figuring out what that actually looks like.

If you saw yourself anywhere in these pages—

in the doubt, the fear, the push and pull—

I hope you give yourself grace.

You're allowed to take your time.

You're allowed to feel everything.

And you're allowed to choose something better...

even if it feels unfamiliar at first.

This story is about putting pieces back together.

Not perfectly—

but honestly.

And sometimes...

that's enough.

Thank you for being here.

For continuing this journey.

For trusting me with these pieces.

— S. Swiss

ACKNOWLEDGMENTS

Book two was never just a continuation—it was healing.

To my readers...

thank you for not letting *Shattered Things* end where it did.

For your messages, your theories, your emotions, and the way you held these characters like they were real. Because to me... they are.

You are the reason I got to tell what comes next.

To those who saw themselves in the broken pieces—

this book is for you.

The ones learning that love after heartbreak doesn't come easy... and that healing isn't linear, pretty, or perfect. But it's possible.

To my family and the people closest to me—

thank you for giving me the space to disappear into this world, even when it took more from me than I expected. Thank you for holding me together when I was writing about falling apart.

To the ones who helped shape this story behind the scenes—

your honesty, your feedback, and your belief in me made this book stronger in every way.

And to the characters who refused to let me stop at the pain—

thank you for showing me that there is something after survival.

That sometimes love comes back quieter... steadier... and real.

This story was never about perfection.

It was about picking up the pieces...

and learning how to hold them together.

With love,

S. Swiss

The Pieces Series

Shattered Things

Some love stories don't end—

they unravel.

Tape and Glue

When everything falls apart,

some things are worth putting back together.

Happily Ever After? September 2026

Because even fairy tales don't promise forever.

The Pieces We Keep (Coming Soon)

Some pieces stay broken.

Others become part of who we are.

www.ingramcontent.com/pod-product-compliance
Lightning Source LLC
Chambersburg PA
CBHW020140170726
47995CB00003BA/646